# TAHARA
# BOY MYSTIC OF INDIA

# TAHARA

*Boy Mystic of India*

*By*

HAROLD M. SHERMAN

THE GOLDSMITH PUBLISHING COMPANY

CHICAGO

# CONTENTS

# Tahara—Boy Mystic of India

## CHAPTER I

## SACRED WATERS

"DICK, just look below there at that mass of humanity! Did you ever see so many human heads in all your life? That old Ganges river is just black with them as far as the eye can see! Boy, what a sight!"

Dan Carter, Dick Oakwood's fat chum and fellow adventurer, pointed downward from the slanting window of the large cabin plane, owned by his father and used for expedition purposes. Here they were at last, over the famous old city of Benares, India, at the time of year when thousands on thousands of pilgrims had come to bathe in the sacred waters of the mighty Ganges, fervently hoping and praying to wash their sins and diseases away.

It had been a torturously hot trip, even by plane, from the land of the Taharans and the wilds of the African continent. A blazing sun now shone mercilessly, affecting birds on the wing as well as humans grovelling on the ground, the earth heat reflecting upward. And all in the cabin of the plane sighed their relief that the long flight was near its end.

There was Professor Hector Oakwood, who had long wanted to visit India for a study of its peoples. And beside him sat Rex Carter, father of the engaging American girl, Ray, and the plump but irrepressible young man who answered to the name of Dan. Mr. Carter had decided many moons ago that this sort of world travel and exploration provided the best possible way of spending his millions. Having financed the expedition originally that his friend, Professor Oakwood, might study a total eclipse of the sun from a vantage point in the desert lands, Mr. Carter had been easily persuaded to remain abroad with the party and aid it in expanding its activities. Now, as he pressed his face against the cabin window, he also directed a remark at the venturesome son of Professor Oakwood who was directly responsible for this flight to India.

"Doesn't look like we can land within miles of here, Dick, without coming down on a field of human skulls! Appears to me you've picked the most congested spot in all India! There's certainly not room for another Hindu in that river! Great heavens! I feel as though I could stand a good bath but this sight is most discouraging. What do you say we turn back? The wilds of Africa were never like this!"

Mr. Carter glanced at Dick, smilingly.

"I never thought there were as many people in the world," Dick admitted.

"The eye of the white brother beholds nothing," spoke Mahatma Sikandar who was seated beside Dick. "India is a harvest of souls ripening through karmic experience. Many must be born, over and over, gaining slow knowledge of the Way, until one life they are awakened to the wisdom of the ages. Then, through their Guru, or teacher, are they led upward to the veil of Peace."

"Not so fast!" begged Dick of the portly wise man, through whose crystal gazing prowess and stories of the great Masters, the exploring party had been led to visit the ancient land of mystery. "I can't digest so much of your occult explanations at one time . . . and I do want to understand it if I can. You don't mean to say these thousands of black heads we see below have been born here many times before?"

Mahatma Sikandar ran a pudgy finger alongside his dark nose. "Not in India alone but in countries long since extinct. Reincarnation, Dick Sahib, is the law of life. You, yourself, have been on earth, not once, but thousands of times!"

Dan Carter, in the seat behind, made a pinwheel motion with his hand, taking care that the Indian seer did not witness him. But the aged Mahatma turned upon him quickly, dark eyes flashing reproachfully.

"So—you do not believe? Dan Sahib is baby soul."

"I didn't say anything," protested Dan, uncomfortably. "And I'm not a baby!"

Dick laughed. "You can't even think with Mahatma around," he joshed.

Across the narrow aisle of the plane, Kurt and Kurul, Dick's two Taharan bodyguards whom he had taken on this new venture, were gazing awesomely at the dark-skinned mystic. They had seen evidence of the Mahatma's powers and feared his magic.

"Mahatma good," Dick reassured them, and they nodded, only half convinced.

The plane suddenly tilted as it swung about and the attention of all was attracted.

"The pilots have sighted a landing field," explained Ray, her brown eyes alight with excitement. "I can hardly wait to get down and see these Hindus at close range!"

"Nothing to 'em except a loin cloth or a bed sheet," sniffed Dan, disrespectfully. "You can see that much from here!"

Ray made an impish face at her brother and exchanged amused glances with Dick. The three made a happy group and had grown to understand each other's temperaments through many thrilling adventures together. Dan particularly had the habit of saying what he didn't mean as a shield to his inner feelings. Dick had an air of abandon about him but was the much more serious and direct of the two. Ray, who had proved her pluck on several hazardous occasions, had a merry, infectious way about her. And now the three were to delve into the ancient world of mysticism. It was to be a new sort of research, this attempt to fathom the powers of the invisible.

"My native country," Mahatma Sikandar was saying, reverently. "It does not change. For years I have been away, but it does not change."

"That's too bad," sympathized Dan, dryly. "Then you won't get any kick out of coming back. I'm glad I've never been here before."

"Dan Sahib is mistaken," insisted Mahatma. "All life is a circle. A straight line becomes curved. You were here hundreds of years ago and now you return."

"It's too much for me," declared Dan, with a gesture of surrender.

The tri-motors of the plane were cut off preparatory to landing and the large aircraft glided down toward the field. It appeared, from above, to be a British airport. Everyone in the party sat quietly as the plane skimmed over a fringe of trees, cleared a row of house-tops and touched its wheels to the levelled off ground.

"Here we are!" announced Dick, as the plane taxied to a stop near a hangar and men in uniform together with dark-skinned attendants came running up.

Greetings were exchanged; official papers were submitted; the freedom of the city was extended Professor Oakwood and his companions, and cars were placed at the disposal of the party to take them to the Crescent Hotel in Benares.

Kurt and Kurul, Dick's Taharan bodyguards, who had been coaxed to take seats in the plane in order that they might fly with the gods, now had to be coaxed all over again to get them in an automobile.

"Auto good," Dick repeated, but Kurt and Kurul stared at the horseless chariot askance, moving away.

"See?" demonstrated Dan, and climbed in one of the cars. "Me not afraid!"

"Who do you think you're talking to?" laughed Ray. "An American Indian?"

Dan's face flushed. "I'm just trying to show those dizzy natives . . ." he started to explain. "I don't see why Dick brought 'em along, anyhow. They're a danged nuisance. Between trying to make them understand us and our trying to savvy the deep stuff Mahatma is passing out, we're going to have brain fag pretty soon!"

"Kurt and Kurul are no worse off than we are when it comes to mysticism," defended Dick, taking his seat in the car beside Dan, and gesturing to the Taharans. "See?" he cried. "Tahara goes . . . You go, Tahara?"

Kurt and Kurul, glancing at one another apprehensively, feared to be left behind more than risking this new steed of motion. The husky Taharans crept into the car and knelt on the floor, clutching the back of the front seat and clinging to it tenaciously. They had acted as delighted as kids when they had become accustomed to plane travel, and the automobile should have been less terrifying except that its speed was more noticeable since it was comparable to the objects flashing past.

For the first few blocks, Kurt and Kurul had to be restrained from jumping out. But they finally relaxed under Dick's renewed assurances and he knew that their instinctive reactions had been quelled when Kurt turned to Kurul with the simple remark: "Auto good!"

For the Taharan warriors who were a survival of the Stone Age races, their transplantation to India was violent. Their limited mentalities were being bombarded by a host of new impressions and it was not to be wondered at that they rebelled until guided by he whom they had accepted as their leader, Dick Oakwood, king of the Taharans!

Benares was swarming with Hindus, people of low and high caste populating the sacred shrines, traveling in all manner of conveyances or on foot to reach the temples and places of worship along the Ganges river. As the two cars bearing Professor Oakwood's party reached the main roadway, progress was all but halted, so impassable were the streets. Dick, Dan and Ray exclaimed again and again in horror or in awe at sights which met their gaze—crumbling ruins of ancient palaces; beggars with twisted limbs and faces, crying for alms; sacred bulls pestered by clouds of flies; squalid dwellings and contrasting buildings of grandeur; a jumbled succession of scenes and people, people and scenes, with the countless legion of dark-skinned worshippers finally seeming to blot out everything else.

Arriving finally at the Crescent Hotel, entrance was made with difficulty due to the merchants, beggars and fakirs who crowded about, making signs and strange mouthings. But Mahatma Sikandar led the way, addressing the throng in Hindustani, and pushing his sleek, over-fat body through a narrow lane, being followed by every member of the party.

"Whew!" gasped Dan when they had reached the hotel lobby and been assigned to rooms. "So this is India! I feel like I'd been dropped into the middle of millions of ants and that they were crawling all over me! Did you ever see such filth? Such ungodly looking creatures? I pity the river Ganges! If cleanliness is next to godliness, that river's got a whale of a job on its hands! I don't know whether I want to eat any food or drink any water in this place or not! Ugh!"

Dick laughed as the party was led upstairs to the second floor where doors were thrown open to rooms, some of which opened out onto balconies overhanging the street from which a far-reaching view could be obtained of the fantastic throngs jostling by.

"Poor Dan," said Dick. "You can stand any discomfort but the loss of appetite. But when you're in Rome, remember the old saying, 'you must do as the Romans!'"

Dan made a wry face. "Say—it would take a Master to do that in this country. After passing those sweetmeat stalls and the market place black with flies, I can't say to my stomach, 'Peace, be still!' . . . No wonder they have outbreaks of plague and cholera! And that Ganges river . . . !"

"They say it's so pure you can drink from it anywhere," reminded Ray, amused at Dan.

"Deliver me!" was her brother's rejoinder. "Can you tell me, Dick, how you expect to find anyone with high spirituality in such surroundings? . . . Why, an American pig wouldn't even live here!"

"*You're* here, aren't you?" joshed Dick.

Dan, grasping his chum, made a move as though to push him over the balcony rail.

Kurt and Kurul, Taharan bodyguards, laid rough hands on Dan at once, scowling and muttering.

"Good night!" groaned Dan, with pretended offense. "I seem to be getting it from all sides!"

"Dan good!" said Dick to his faithful Taharans. "Let him go! Dan good!"

Kurt and Kurul released Dan but still frowned upon him. Their dog-like loyalty to the person they regarded as ruler had protected Dick in moments of real danger in the past. These Taharan warriors would not even trust Dan Carter until his motives were understood.

"I guess you'll let me alone hereafter," smiled Dick. "You wondered a while ago why I brought Kurt and Kurul along. Isn't this a good reason? They'd protect our whole party if I ordered it . . . and you can't tell what we may run into here."

"A lot of good they'll be against Master minds," disparaged Dan. "This Mahatma Sikandar has got 'em petrified right now. All he has to do is turn those black eyes of his on 'em and their knees bang together."

"That may be," admitted Dick, "but everyone in India isn't a Master mind, thank goodness. Besides, I want to test these primitive minds out against Master minds. They ought to make the greatest contrast in the world!"

Dan stared at Dick for a moment. "If you don't get some of the craziest ideas!" he finally blurted. "Next thing I know you'll be looking for the missing link . . . or maybe you think these ginks *are* the missing link?"

"I think they *are* close to it," said Dick.

To which Dan replied, with a helpless shrug of the shoulders: "There you are! I give up! This whole business is beyond me! But, brother, what I'd give for some good old-fashioned ham and eggs! Or if you can't get that, go out and kill a sacred bull . . . !"

"Careful!" warned Dick, looking about him quickly, his face sobering. "That's something you can't do, Dan, make fun of the Indian religion. A crack like that might get us all in trouble!"

Even as Dick spoke, a turbaned Indian, on a balcony across the street, turned and stared intently. Dan, following Dick's eyes, wheeled slowly and ventured a look. His face paled.

"Do you suppose he heard what I said?" he whispered.

"I don't know," replied Dick, concernedly. "But don't ever make a thoughtless remark like that again. These people take their worship very seriously; they would gladly die for their religion, and while they are supposed to be exceedingly charitable to others, I wouldn't want to invite their ill will. There's a certain something about them . . ."

"You said it," rejoined Dan, moistening dry lips. "A certain something that gives you a creepy feeling. Look at that guy over there! He's standing like a statue, arms folded. What's he trying to do—hypnotize us?"

"I think we'd better step inside," Dick advised, a bit uneasily. "Perhaps Mahatma can tell us something about him."

Kurt and Kurul, noting the sudden anxiety on Dick's face, followed him with inquiring gestures. But Dick led them across the hall and pointed out a small back room which they were to occupy. He indicated that they were to remain until he called them.

Going next to the room which had been assigned to Mahatma Sikandar, Dick rapped on the door.

"No answer," Dick said to Dan, after a moment. "And the door is locked."

"Maybe he's in concentration," suggested Dan.

"Boost me up," whispered Dick. "I'll look through the crack at the top of the door and see."

Dan grasped his chum about the waist and hoisted him.

"He's not in his room," said Dick. "Perhaps he's in the front room with Dad and your father."

But Professor Oakwood and Rex Carter, who had been busy unpacking the things they were going to need, reported they had not seen Mahatma since they had come upstairs.

"He's no doubt gone out, looking up old acquaintances," said the Professor. "What did you want him for?"

"Nothing particular," said Dick, and glanced guardedly at Dan.

Just then a knock sounded on the door and

Ray came in. Her usually bright face was shadowed with fright.

"There's a man in a balcony across the street who's been staring at me," she informed. "I stepped to my window to look out and his eyes caught mine. I don't know how to describe it but I had the awfullest time drawing away from him. It seemed as though he were pulling me to him."

Dan placed a protecting arm about the trembling form of his sister.

"It's the same guy," he said to Dick. Then, excitedly, to his father. "Look across on that balcony, Dad! There's a Hindu over there who's trying black magic on us!"

Professor Oakwood and Rex Carter hurried to their own balcony and glanced across the street as directed. They turned back, puzzled.

"You young people must be seeing things," scolded Professor Oakwood. "There's no one there."

"But there was!" insisted Dick. "A dark-skinned man in white turban and blue flowing garment."

"If there was," said Rex Carter, lightly, "there isn't now. I'm afraid you're all working your imaginations over time. You're ready to believe that any Hindu who looks at you has the power of mesmerism. Don't let these new surroundings and new people excite you."

Dan, Ray and Dick exchanged somewhat sheepish glances. Perhaps they had been too impressed by a man who appeared unduly interested in them. And yet it was strange that Ray should have gotten the same uncanny reaction without any suggestion from them.

"Maybe we're goofy," Dan conceded, "but I've been looked at by plenty of funny people and I've never felt like I did when that bozo put his glimmers on me."

"I'd like to spot him again," said Dick, determinedly.

"*I* wouldn't," said Ray, shuddering.

## Chapter II

## THE CRYSTAL FOREWARNS

Sight-seeing in Benares occupied the time and thoughts of all in the party for the next several days. Hours were spent at the water-front watching the thousands of worshippers entering the river Ganges, submerging themselves in the Mother, as the water was lovingly called, and going through the ritual of dedicating their souls to the Giver of Life. There was an ecstacy and a devotion about these consecrating Hindus which commanded respect, particularly when it was recalled that this ceremony had been going on for some five thousand years.

"Once would be enough for me," observed Dan, with a grimace. "Just look at these heathens . . . !"

"Dan, you mustn't call them that!" cautioned Ray, poking him.

"Well, that's what they are!" said Dan.

"And after all this worship, what has their God done for them? Most of 'em are poor and scrawny and undernourished and crippled and blind and bowlegged and ... jiminy whiz, I never saw such a hodgepodge of humans in my life! Can you explain why they're like that, Dick, unless their God doesn't want to make them any better because He figures they wouldn't worship Him if there was nothing the matter?"

Dick shook his head, thoughtfully. This spectacle had aroused questions within which he himself could not answer.

"You've got me there, Dan. I guess, if we knew the reason for all this, we'd be Masters ourselves!"

Dan grunted. "It makes me mighty glad I'm who I am, anyhow!" he commented.

"And just *who* is that?" asked Dick, pointedly.

"What do you mean?" demanded Dan, after a moment. "I don't get you."

"I mean," explained Dick, "that you and I don't actually know who we are. We came into this life and our parents gave us the names of Dan Carter and Dick Oakwood . . . but if our names were taken away from us tomorrow, we'd still have the same identity . . . the same '*I am*' consciousness within!"

Dan stared hard as he thought Dick's comment over.

"That's right!" he breathed, greatly impressed. "I'd never thought of that. My name is not myself, is it? It's just a convenient handle by which others know me! Holy smoke—a few thoughts like that and a guy could go bughouse!"

Dick grinned. "A few thoughts like that and a guy would begin to *think!*" he corrected.

"I never knew before that I didn't know who I was!" Dan repeated to himself. "Now you've got me all balled up. I wish you hadn't mentioned that at all. I didn't come here to study mysticism. I came here to see India . . . and I've already gotten more than an eyeful. Let's move on!"

But Dan was more interested than he would admit, and so was Ray, his sister. Ray objected to being left at the hotel on special trips about the town where men might ordinarily have gone alone. Wherever possible, however revolting the sights, Ray wished to be taken. And her father, Rex Carter, laughingly typifying her as a girl adventurer, had granted permission declaring that a few such trips would "cure" her. But in this he had been wrong; Ray was more eager than ever to "see all" as she expressed it, "and know all."

Since their first day in the hotel when the Hindu in the balcony across the street had stared so hypnotically at Dan, Dick and Ray, no trace of him had been seen. Mahatma Sikandar, returning after some hours, had laughed at their stories of apprehension.

"Why shouldn't one of my race gaze in rapture at so beautiful a white girl?" had been Mahatma's rejoinder to Ray's account. And then, as Rex Carter's attractive daughter had blushed prettily, the aged crystal gazer had added: "We do not see so many girls of your type in India. You must expect to be looked at. And you must remember, most Indian woman, even today, are scarcely permitted in public. That is, the women who . . ."

"I understand," said Ray, cutting him short.

For some reason, Ray had not liked Mahatma's prying eyes. To her he had seemed to be saying one thing and thinking another. True, he had shown every friendliness for the members of the party and had been helpful in piloting them around. Everyone depended upon Mahatma to make arrangements, to express their wants, and to suggest additional trips to places of interest. Mahatma, because he had not been Master enough, as Dan had facetiously remarked, to keep his weight down, had tactfully seen to it that their sight-seeing required as little walking as possible. And Mahatma Sikandar, himself, with a certain sense of humor, had declared that his size had compelled him to develop the ability to travel in his mind instead of transporting his body.

"This bird who looked at my sister, wouldn't have had the same excuse to look at me," protested Dan. "So your explanation doesn't hold water there, Mahatma. I'm no prize beauty and yet he gave me the 'evil eye' or something like it. How do you explain that?"

"You were too excited over India," replied Mahatma, his tongue in a fat cheek. "You need to develop self-control, Dan Sahib. Then the eyes of a stranger, they are meaningless."

But Dan remained unconvinced. And even after some days had passed, he found himself searching in the crowds, starting suddenly as he thought himself confronted with the Hindu in question, and stealing glances at the balcony across the street from the hotel, half anticipating to see the figure of the man there again.

"I guess," Dan said finally to Dick, "that Mahatma was right. You and I were 'seeing' things that first day. If that bird had been bent on causing us any trouble, don't you suppose we'd have heard from him by now?"

Dick shook his head. "Can't prove it by me," was his reply. "These Indians have a different conception of time than we. They can wait years to accomplish their desires. And if that Hindu really had any intentions . . ."

"What are you trying to do?" demanded Dan, forcing a grin. "Spoil my appetite?"

Professor Oakwood had been captivated by the ancient architecture of the Hindus as represented by their strange and marvelous temples, shrines and tombs—often scooped from the living rock of caves, hills or built of stone with high pyramidal towers, fantastically ornamented.

"I want to make a study of these wonders," said Dick's father. "They interest me more than a search for Fakirs."

Dick grinned. "That's where you and I differ, Dad. You're more interested in the physical accomplishments of a people and I am more interested in the people themselves . . ."

"How fortunate!" was Professor Oakwood's amiable answer. "Then between us we should acquire a rather complete knowledge of every country we visit."

"Suits me," accepted Dick, "if you'll grant me freedom to explore as I like."

"Have I ever interfered with your activities?" smiled the Professor. "How many fathers would have granted a son such free reign as you had with that Taharan tribe? I've never had to worry about you, Dick. You learned early how to take care of yourself and you've done a mighty good job of it."

Dick was naturally pleased at his father's profession of confidence.

"While compliments are being thrown around," was his rejoinder, "I might say that I owe what little I know to your training. And if I ever amount to anything as a scientist . . ."

But Professor Oakwood, equally pleased at his son's appraisal of him, dismissed the subject with an airy wave of the hand.

The holy city of India, containing an almost infinite allure, held the party fascinated. While Professor Oakwood and Rex Carter were examining the decorative interior of a sacred shrine or temple, Dan, Ray, Dick and Mahatma Sikandar would be roaming the streets, searching out odd characters and interviewing them. The Mahatma was indispensable on such trips, his translating of the tongues spoken giving Dick the opportunity to learn much. Many natives, however, refused to be drawn into conversation. Some would sit quietly in the narrow streets near the river front, staring kindly but unanswering. In these canyon-like streets no modern vehicle could go, and the trio of American youths were forced to thread their way amid a never-ending flow of bewildered looking pilgrims making the rounds of the sacred road, Panch-kos, that they might be cleansed of their sins.

Kurt and Kurul, accompanying Dick on most of his ramblings, attracted much attention, the Indians realizing that they were gazing upon men from a primitive race. The Taharans strode beside Dick like faithful dogs, watching their King in every move he made and appealing to him for reassurance whenever something they could not understand aroused their terror.

To every native interviewed, whether beggar or high-caste banker, Dick had Mahatma Sikandar direct the one all-important question: "The American Sahib wishes to know where he may find a guru or teacher of the immortal truths."

But in every instance, this question was met with silence.

"Funny people," observed Dan. "Most religious race I've ever seen and yet when you ask them where to locate one of their Master minds, they act like you'd committed the unpardonable sin."

"It is a law," Mahatma Sikandar explained. "No pupil or student may mention the name of his Master. I could have told Dick Sahib but one learns best through experience."

"Then how are we going to get next to the guys who walk through fire, climb up ropes into space, and cut babies in two?" asked Dan, disappointed. "I think its all bologney . . ."

"What does the white brother say?" Mahatma demanded of Dick.

"Bologney is the American word for *myth*," laughed Dick. "Dan is slightly incredulous . . ." And then, as he saw their Indian guide still frowning, he added: "Dan doesn't believe in Hindu magic. He must be shown. And since he hasn't seen any of these wonders, he's doubtful as to whether they really exist."

Mahatma Sikandar gave an agitated grunt.

"In this country, one must be worthy or things are not revealed. When the pupil is ready, the teacher appears."

"But what can we do to get ready?" persisted Ray. "Could a girl ever become a Yogi?"

"There have been women," answered Mahatma, mysteriously, "who have sat in high places."

"We'll take you up in the mountains," kidded Dan. "That's all you need, Sis, for development."

Ray's face flushed. The mysteries of India had interested her as much as they had intrigued Dan and Dick. But, beyond the religious fervor she had witnessed in the places of worship and with the throngs who bathed in the river Ganges, nothing actually inexplainable had occurred except, perhaps, the man on the balcony who had gazed so intently upon her . . . ! There had been Mahatma Sikandar, of course, and his crystal ball, but even this had failed to impress her particularly since their Indian seer had been able to verify very little of that which he had reported.

"I wonder," Ray had confided to Dick, "if Mahatma is fooling us with his crystal gazing? It's gotten him a good job in our employ and

a trip back to his native country. But sometimes I think that Mahatma is bluffing . . . that
he's just acting mysterious . . . and that he
doesn't possess the powers we imagine he has.
He may have been able to hoodwink the blacks
in Africa but now that he's back among his own
people . . ."

"He has a certain telepathic ability, I'm certain," said Dick, cutting her short. "And I'm
sure he could hypnotize if he cared to. But
Mahatma never claimed he could put us in
touch with the real wise men of India. He
knows he's not developed enough to do that. I
think the old boy's okay as far as he's
gone. Why have you taken such a dislike to
him?"

"I don't know," said Ray, trying to analyze
her own feelings. "Maybe he's gotten on my
nerves after my one experience with that
Hindu who almost put me under his spell.
Every time those black eyes of Mahatma look
at me, I feel uncomfortable. But I'm trying
not to let him know how I feel against him."

Ray, whose own eyes were dark beneath
her black, curly hair, looked anxiously at Dick.

She respected his judgment and his confidence much more than that of her carefree brother, Dan. Dick's nerves were steady; he wasn't easily stampeded, and he had the faculty of thinking things through. If Dick considered Mahatma Sikandar all right, then she shouldn't let the old crystal gazer get on her nerves.

"If you think ill of Mahatma, he'll sense it," said Dick, "so you're wise, Ray, in deciding to drop your suspicions. Mahatma is a bit conceited about his powers and likes to be given credit for everything he does, which is not the mark of the Master. But so long as he serves us satisfactorily, I feel we should play up to him."

And this advice was followed, Mahatma Sikandar apparently appreciating the adulation paid him, extending his fat and ordinarily lazy self to help them realize their desires.

One rainy night when none but the pilgrims were out, making *puja* or worship before their shrines, Dick suggested to Mahatma that he sit before his crystal and see if he could detect what the immediate future might have in store. Mahatma demurred at first but, on urging from Dan and Ray, finally consented.

"Conditions are not good," he complained as he took up the crystal ball which he kept concealed in a large black silk cloth. "When I look, desiring to see, nothing comes. But when I look, expecting nothing, something comes. You must be patient."

"We will be," promised Dan, the least likely of the three to meet the requirement. "Go ahead, brother! Do your stuff!"

This was hardly the way to admonish an Indian seer but Mahatma had gradually accustomed himself to Dan Sahib's impulsive albeit slightly irreverent manner, and paid no heed beyond a reproving grunt as he prepared to gaze into the crystal.

Ray, Dan and Dick seated themselves about the little table at which Mahatma sat, leaning his elbows upon it, the crystal held in his plump, dark-skinned fingers. He polished the glass ball with the black silk cloth, then concentrated his eyes upon it. Minutes ticked past and the aged crystal gazer had not moved, nor had any of the trio detected so much as a flicker of his eyelids. Dan, who found it difficult to sit still long at a time, was growing decidedly uncomfortable and ill at ease. Ray and Dick, however, were too interested in studying Mahatma to be conscious of their own feelings.

"Kerchoo!"

Dan couldn't help himself, the sneeze had taken him unawares.

"I'm sorry," he apologized as Mahatma lowered the crystal ball. "I suppose that spoiled the . . . er . . . vibrations?"

"I was just entering the white cloud of vision," said Mahatma. "The formless was about to take form. If Dan Sahib's nose still offends, perhaps he had best absent himself . . ."

"No," decided Dan, with an appealing glance at Ray and Dick. "I want to see this thing through. I guarantee not to break up your show again."

So saying, Dan took out a handkerchief with which to smother any further disturbance. And Ray and Dick settled back once more as Mahatma returned to his crystal gazing.

Outside could be heard the incessant patter of rain which increased the shut-in feeling and added to the suspense as Mahatma Sikandar's eyes suddenly widened and he gave evidence at last of seeing something in the polished crystal.

"The cloud lifts," Mahatma announced, peering intently. "There is a scene by the Golden Temple. All is confusion. Dick Sahib is in trouble!"

"Me—in trouble?" spoke up Dick, quickly. "What kind of trouble?"

"I cannot quite see," replied Mahatma, rubbing the black cloth over the crystal as though to make the vision clearer. "But it has something to do with the sacred monkeys . . ."

Dan grinned. "Maybe Dick pulled one of their tails," he suggested.

"Don't, Dan!" protested Ray, pinching his arm. "Be serious, can't you?"

"What connection could I possibly have with sacred monkeys?" Dick asked, wonderingly.

Mahatma Sikandar gazed into the crystal for a moment, a deep furrowed frown on his fat face.

"Dick Sahib has two subjects from Tahara.

It is they who will cause him the trouble."

"Kurt and Kurul?" stated Dick, incredulously.

Mahatma nodded. "I see a priest talking to Dick Sahib. The priest is very angry. He points to his sacred monkeys and then to the Sahib's bodyguard and what he says makes you feel . . . what shall I say? . . . sick and faint in the stomach! . . . I feel like you will feel as I see what is written in the future for you!"

Dick exchanged a consulting glance with Ray who, impressed by Mahatma Sikandar's recital, broke in with an anxious question.

"And what is this trouble going to lead to?"

"That I cannot see," replied the aged crystal gazer. "Except that you will all be in danger . . ."

"Now you're talking!" spoke up Dan, showing sudden interest. "Things have begun to get monotonous compared to our usual run of experience . . . and if there's going to be some excitement, me for it!"

Mahatma Sikandar looked up, shaking his head, soberly.

"Dan Sahib speaks with a fool's tongue. Before another sun has set, he will have the sentence of death passed upon him!"

Dan blinked his eyes for a moment, then attempted to laugh it off.

"Ho, ho! You think you can scare me, Mahatma? You've put on a pretty good show. It's worth a couple of rupees of any man's money." And Dan made a motion toward his pocket.

Mahatma Sikandar held up his hand. He had not been averse to accepting coin since his joining of Professor Oakwood's party, but this time he refused.

"The crystal does not lie. It has forewarned. Dan Sahib had best pray to his white God. Dick Sahib also. The time is short!"

Ray, who had been given to doubting the aged crystal gazer, could not deny his apparent sincerity in this instance.

"Is this all you can tell us?" she begged. "It is still so vague. If we knew more exactly what to look for . . .?"

"I see no more," said Mahatma Sikandar, covering his crystal ball with the black cloth. "The future has spoken . . ."

A minute followed in which the dreary sound of the rain seemed unbearable. Here the three were, hemmed in by something ominous, something approaching out of the invisible, a something which Mahatma Sikandar, with his psychic sight, had glimpsed in a shaft of future time! His prophesy was unbelievable, of course, almost ridiculous! But, then, the Indian seer had made other predictions, none quite so alarming as this, and they had come generally true. It all couldn't be ascribed to guess work or shrewd calculation. Mahatma's vision had curiously involved Kurt and Kurul which had given the whole impression a touch of the fantastic when the matter was linked up with sacred monkeys.

"It's too much for me," said Dan, finally, after Mahatma had retired, leaving the three to discuss the result of his crystal gazing. "It sounds to me like the kind of impressions that would run through my mind after mixing lobsters with pickled pig's feet."

"I can't figure the thing out, either," Dick admitted, "but I don't think we should take Mahatma's warning too lightly."

"By all means," seconded Ray.

"Before another sun sets," reflected Dan, "we're to be under a death sentence! . . . Hmmm! . . . Say, Dick, you got any more of that funny Hindu candy left?"

# Chapter III

## A CURSE IS UTTERED

India's rain which bathed the landscape as the faithful river Ganges had been bathing its changing population, had abated by morning and a warm sun was shining over the ghats already black with worshippers prostrating themselves in the temples and upon the descending steps which led to the water's edge. Every day a veritable Sunday in Benares!

And Dick, arising early, desired to mingle again with the throngs, studying the endless array of types, seeking anew some hint that might lead to the abode of a Master. It was easy enough to find a cheap fakir or a native who had performed such feats of asceticism as holding one arm aloft until it had become shrunken and rigid. There were also many men and women who had sat in one position for so long, legs doubled beneath them, that the lower limbs were crippled. Such sights were common and yet, to Dick, these strange people demonstrated no unusual power of mind except a stolid adherence to certain religious principles which, to a class of Hindus, seemed a normal way of living. Dick desired to contact a man of India far above this spiritual plane, if such types actually existed; if they were not just a part of the folklore of this most mysterious of countries. Mahatma Sikandar had assured Dick that such men were not myths; that they did exist, some in mountain fastnesses, others in desert monasteries; but rarely did they reveal themselves, even when they, disguised as ordinary natives, mingled with the seething millions of India's suffering populace.

"What do you say, Dan?" Dick proposed, "to another day amid the baths?"

"Well, if you want to know the truth," was Dan's rejoinder, "I'm getting tired of the holy city and that goes for the sacred bulls, the sacred monkeys and the funny holy men who run around next to naked all smeared with ashes. This place is like a circus—if you've seen it once, you've seen it all."

"I don't agree with you," opposed Dick. "Each day is a new day with me—and it would be for you, too, if you looked for people instead of things . . ."

Dan rubbed a spot behind his ear a bit sheepishly. Then his face suddenly lit up.

"Say, I'd almost forgot. This is the day, according to our goofy crystal gazer, that we're supposed to meet our doom. That being the case, I'll go with you!"

Dick smiled. "You *that* anxious to meet your doom?"

"No—but you'll have to admit it'll be *different*," was Dan's reply.

Ray, however, on learning Dick's plans and being invited to go along, hung back uncertainly.

"Are you sure you *should* go?" she questioned. "Perhaps it would be better if you lounged about the hotel today."

Dan laughed and patted his sister reassuringly on the shoulder.

"Now, Sis—you don't mean to confess that you've taken Mahatma *that* seriously? We'll probably have him explaining to us tonight after nothing's happened, that his vision was symbolic."

"I suppose it is a little foolish," Ray conceded. "But there's no real reason, is there, of us going near the Golden Temple?"

"What's wrong with it?" Dan wanted to know.

"Why, that's where Mahatma said the trouble was going to start," explained Ray, her face coloring.

"Fine!" welcomed Dan, "then that's just the spot we want to head for, eh, Dick?"

But Dick was not so impulsively inclined.

"We should be able to counteract Mahatma's prediction easily enough," he declared, thoughtfully. "Mahatma said Kurt and Kurul were going to be mixed up in the difficulty. But they *can't* be if we leave them here at the hotel!"

"Good idea!" approved Ray. "Why don't you step across the hall now and tell Kurt and Kurul that they're to remain in their room today?"

"I'll do it," Dick decided.

He found Kurt and Kurul eagerly awaiting

his coming. On making known his request, however, the two Taharans scowled deeply, unable to understand why they should not and could not accompany him.

"Tahara Master may need us," pleaded Kurt.

"We promise Raal to protect our King," added Kurul. "Let us go with you, oh, Master!"

"Not today," said Dick, moved by the loyalty and concern shown by the Taharans over his safety. "The gods will protect your King and they command that you wait here for your Master. Is that clear?"

Kurt and Kurul nodded, their faces registering disappointment and uneasiness. Dick stepped out, closing the door upon them. He hesitated a moment before returning to Dan and Ray. Was he doing the right thing by leaving Kurt and Kurul behind? He had become so accustomed to their protection, even though it had been necessary to watch them almost as much as they had watched him, to prevent their groundless terror over things they could not comprehend. But now that

Dick contemplated a trip without Kurt and Kurul tagging along, particularly in the light of Mahatma's prediction, he felt a twinge of his nerves. India was steeped in a fatalistic atmosphere. There was a 'what is to be, will be' attitude on the part of the natives who believed in reincarnation, that a soul returns again and again in an earthly body to atone for past sins or mistakes, until it finally has learned the lessons of life and earned for itself a higher abode in the realms of spirit.

"I shouldn't let myself feel this way," Dick decided. "We came to this country for adventure and exploration and it's developments like this that should make it interesting."

Ray and Dan were ready to go when Dick rejoined them.

"How did Kurt and Kurul take it?" Ray asked.

"All right," Dick informed, not wishing to alarm her. "My subjects always obey me."

"Your're not, by any chance, meaning to include Dan and me in that statement?" teased Ray, her dark eyes flashing.

"I wouldn't dare," laughed Dick, paying

compliment to the girl whose courageous spirit and cheery nature he had grown to respect. "A king always takes orders from the Queen!"

Ray blushed prettily and bowed her dark, curly head.

"Here, here!" broke in Dan, mockingly. "The court jester can't stand for anything like this. A king and queen making eyes at each other! What's this country coming to?"

So saying, Dan grasped Ray and Dick by the arm, propelling them down the stairs and out onto the street where they were immediately lost in the eternal stream of pilgrims, being borne, unresisting, toward "Mother Gunga," the ancient and honorable river Ganges . . . at a point where the human stream mingled with the water of waters.

Mahatma Sikandar had been retained for the day by Professor Oakwood and Rex Carter to aid in their own observations which had left Ray, Dan and Dick to shift for themselves. They had preferred such an arrangement on this occasion since they wanted to be certain, if anything did happen, that they had not been led into it by the old crystal gazer.

"If Mahatma had come with us," said Dan, "I'd have been suspicious of any occurrence, that he'd framed it in advance. But now there's no chance of any collusion. We're out entirely on our own and you can't tell me that things can be figured ahead of time. If they are, it's only because the person predicting 'em has the physical power to make 'em happen or some perfectly explainable inside information that they're going to take place."

Ray shook her head, debatingly. "But how could Mahatma get any knowledge in advance of how sacred monkeys would get mixed up with Kurt and Kurul and cause us trouble?"

Dan grinned. "It hasn't happened yet, has it?" he demanded.

"N—no," admitted Ray.

"Then that's the answer," retorted Dan, smugly. "And it isn't going to happen. There's strange things in India all right—that guy with the hypnotic eyes for one . . . but there's a limit to what these babies can do—and I'm not at all convinced that . . ."

The three had been wandering more or less aimlessly, enjoying anew the spectacle of the city's outline from the waterfront. Benares, a city which had existed years before London and Paris were thought of . . . whose temples, mosques, palaces, domes and minarets formed a curious, highly colored jamble along the steep banks of the river.

Many of the human sights were as loathsome as the physical sight was inspiring. And the day, unusually crowded with interesting incidents, drew toward its close with nothing untoward having occurred.

"That old sun's going to be set in another hour or so," observed Dan, dryly. "And we're not under death sentence yet!"

Ray and Dick could take the prophecy lightly now. In fact, Mahatma's dire warning had slipped their minds for the better part of the day, so absorbed had they been at watching such events as the cremation of a corpse on one of the "burning ghats," with attendant religious rites as the soul, thus cleansed by the flames, had been liberated to its next phase of existence before entering once more the karmic wheel of progression. Every sight had called for its spiritual interpretation which Ray, Dan and Dick had obtained sometimes, only with difficulty—and sometimes not at all. But now they were bound back to the hotel Crescent where Dick was anxious to transcribe certain rough notes he had made into a permanent record while the incidents were still fresh in his mind.

Of a sudden, as they were passing one of the temples, piercing screams rang out and a commotion became apparent among worshippers of all classes.

"Hello!" exclaimed Dan. "Some excitement for a change! Let's see what's up!"

And, forthwith, Dan started forward as the natives, gesticulating and crying, arms raised above their heads, came pouring from the temple.

"These screams don't sound human!" gasped Ray.

"They're not," recognized Dick, his face turning pale. "It's the terror cry of outraged *monkeys!*"

"Monkeys!" repeated Dan, and looked sidewise at Dick. "Well, it's a good thing you left Kurt and Kurul at the hotel. They might have gotten mixed up with this fracas, at that!"

"Indeed they might!" added Ray, excitedly. "Have you noticed?   It's the Golden Temple that Mahatma saw in his crystal!"

Dan and Dick gasped.

"It can't be!" said Dan, unbelievingly.

"It is!" verified Dick, "there's only one Golden Temple in Benares!"

"Then come on," decided Dan, grabbing Dick by the arm.   "Let's be getting out of here!"

"Not so fast," counselled Dick.   "I want to check on Mahatma's impression.   He apparently got part of it right . . . that part about the monkeys . . . and our being near the Golden Temple when it happened . . . but I don't get our connection to this thing at all, except as eye witnesses . . ."

Dick's attitude served to calm Ray and Dan and the three pressed forward even closer to determine, if possible, the cause of the disturbance.   As they did so, several priests could be discerned, driving two figures before them. In the arms of these figures, shrieking, biting and scratching, were a pair of sacred monkeys.

"Dick!" cried Dan, his eyes bulging. "Am I *seeing* things?   Have we been hypnotized ... or is that really ... ?"

"It's *Kurt* and *Kurul!*" identified Dick, his heart seeming to stop beating.

Ray placed a hand to her pulsating throat. It was as though she was unwillingly enacting a scene that she had gone through before in greater detail.   How could Kurt and Kurul possibly have gotten into the Temple?   How did they happen to be passing the place at this instant?   How did the monkeys get involved with the two primitive-minded Taharans? And how completely was Mahatma Sikandar's uncanny vision to be carried out?

While these questions were flashing through Ray's numbed mind, Dick had sprung into action.   Pushing ahead through the scattering natives, he reached the side of the harassed Kurt and Kurul.   As he did so, Kurt, having grasped his sacred monkey by the throat, gave its neck a quick jerk and flung the animal from him. Its body landed among a group of horrified worshippers who set up a loud lamentation. Kurul, about to dispatch the monkey he held in the same manner, was restrained by Dick who, the moment the animal was released, saw it go hobbling piteously and leap into the arms of a priest. An angry mob then closed in upon the party and Dick, addressing Kurt and Kurul, demanded to know, in their language, the meaning of all this; why they had disobeyed him in leaving the hotel, and why this savage behavior?

"We wait and wait for our king!" an agitated Kurt tried to explain in his tongue. "He no come back. We go hunt for him. We look and look and look. We think we see our king go in here so we follow. We want to look around. They try to put us out. The monkeys they jump on us . . . they scratch and they bite . . . we grab them . . . then everybody start making noise . . . we are attacked . . . we fight back . . . we think they got our king and won't give him up . . . so we take their monkeys . . ."

"You shouldn't have done that!" reprimanded Dick, grasping each by an arm. "You have done a great wrong!"

"Stand back! Let these two alone!" cried

Dan, forcing his way in beside Dick and offering belligerent protection to the Taharans. His sharp commands were not understood by many of the highly incensed worshippers who screamed out their hatred of the primitive men and their white brothers who were trying to defend them.

"Keep your head, Dan!" Dick appealed. "This is a bad mess. Where's Ray? We must look out for her . . . can't tell what's going to be the outcome of this!"

"I'm right here behind you," spoke up Ray. She had been submitting to little indignities hurled at her from the lower caste Hindus, some of whom spat upon her to show their irritation at the desecration of the Golden Temple. But Ray had disregarded the molestations, concerned not so much for herself as the jeopardy in which her brother and Dick had been placed.

"I'm terribly sorry," Dick addressed to the priests, one of whom had recovered the body of the dead sacred monkey and was caressing it with soft and mournful utterings. "These two beings knew no better," Dick tried to explain. "They're related to the Stone-Age tribes, one of the earliest civilizations. They misunderstood . . . am I making myself clear? Does any one of you speak English?"

One of the priests, an emaciated ascetic in whose eyes gleamed the fire of seeming ages, nodded.

"I understand too well, Sahib," he said, speaking slowly, deliberately, and with an ominous note in his voice. "We, of India, have room for only the sincere seekers after Truth. We resent impostors, cheap foreigners who come to loot our temples of their treasures, to despoil the things we hold sacred, and to make a mockery of our worship."

"But that's not our attitude or intention," interrupted Dick. "Won't you let me explain further? I'm sure if you do . . . ?"

"The law of retribution is just," continued the priest, unmoved by Dick's appeal. "Therefore, hear my curse!"

Lifting a thin, bony hand toward the setting sun, the priest solemnly invoked the wrath of his god. Ray, Dan and Dick, standing helpless, surrounded by strange and unsympathetic faces, heard the curse with commingled feelings of horror and anxiety.

"Within a week from this day one of you will be dead; within another week, another will be dead; within yet a third week, death shall strike three times. I have spoken."

A moment followed, a torturous, breathless moment, broken only by the whimpering of the surviving sacred monkey. Then Dan found his voice as he cried out: "But you can't do this! We didn't mean any harm! You can't punish us for what these Taharans did! That's not justice!"

"I have spoken," the priest repeated, fixing his eyes rigidly upon Dan. "You will go quickly!"

The priest made a gesture of dispersal with a skinny arm and the crowd of worshippers, interpreting his meaning, muttered at the unfortunate trio in various tongues. To remain was decidedly unhealthy and Dick, pushing a subdued Kurt and Kurul before him, beckoned to Dan and Ray to follow.

"Mahatma was right," was the first remark Dan made when they had gotten some distance from the Golden Temple. "I take it all back. That guy *can* read the future—he reads it too darn well!"

"What are we going to do?" asked Ray, tremulously.

"That's what I'm trying to decide," said Dick, soberly. "Apparently if a thing is going to happen, you can't do much to prevent it."

"Not in this country, anyhow," agreed Dan, mournfully. "In America we'd call what's just happened to us 'being put on the spot.' Over here, the only difference is, they don't name the spot . . . and you can't tell what to look out for. Say, I'm commencing to get goose pimples!"

"We're in for it now and no mistake," Dick confided, in a low tone so that Ray would not hear. "We've been in tight places together before, Dan, but I've a feeling that we're nearer death this minute than we've ever been in the past."

"You don't mean it?" gasped Dan, looking about concernedly.

"I do," said Dick, quietly but with conviction. "I've heard it said that once a Hindu utters a curse, nothing on earth can save his intended victim."

Dan gulped unpleasantly. "Looks like the only thing for us to do is leave the country."

Dick shook his head. "That won't help. You can't run away from it. The curse will get you at the prescribed time—*any* place."

The three, with Kurt and Kurul walking ahead, turned into the street leading to their hotel.

"And I laughed at this stuff!" Dan mumbled, finally. "Well, at this rate, it looks like the Hindus are going to have the *last* laugh . . ."

"It certainly does," said Dick between tight lips. "Dan, we've got to fight this thing . . . just how I don't know! But we've got to fight!"

Dan gave a helpless shrug of his shoulders. "How are you going to fight anything you can't see?" he asked.

And to this there was no answer.

# Chapter IV

## MYSTERY BECKONS

Ray, Dan and Dick held a brief conference before walking in upon Rex Carter and Professor Oakwood to determine whether they would tell their fathers of this mysterious danger which threatened. It was decided that this was one peril which they could and should not keep to themselves. The counsel of a scientist and explorer, such as Professor Oakwood, was particularly needed, not to mention such occult advice as it was hoped that Mahatma Sikandar might be able to give since he had demonstrated his power to foresee the event. And after the three had given their individual versions of the affair, two extremely concerned older men called a round table discussion in an effort to hit upon a means of combating the curse.

"Mahatma," addressed Professor Oakwood, "you should know how to deal with this situation. What can we do about it? We'll stop at nothing, it goes without saying, to counteract the possible effects of the curse."

The aged crystal gazer sat motionless, his chin resting on a fat hand. He seemed to be staring into space with a peculiar fixedness. All in the party remained silent awaiting Mahatma's answer. There was an air of tenseness, so much so that a book, suddenly knocked off the table by Professor Oakwood's elbow caused all to jump.

"Mahatma is sorry," the Indian seer who had acted as guide to the party finally declared, with apparent reluctance, "but he sees no way. All appears to be darkness ahead."

Dan gave a low whistle and ran a hand nervously through his hair.

"Better try your crystal again," he suggested. "You might be able to see something brighter."

But Mahatma Sikandar shook his head.

"It would do no good. Mahatma is powerless to see more—the curse forbids."

Rex Carter drummed his fingers worriedly on the table.

"Perhaps if I looked up the priest I could buy off his curse," he proposed. "Couldn't I make an offering to his temple? I'd give any reasonable figure."

"Carter Sahib may try," assented the old crystal gazer, gloomily. "But Mahatma is sorry to have to say—very little chance."

"Nevertheless, I'll visit the temple the first thing in the morning," decided Rex Carter. "And I want you, Mahatma, to go with me. You must help me reason with this fanatical priest. We must get him to withdraw his curse. The man can't have meant what he said. I can understand his desiring to wreak vengeance upon Kurt and Kurul but for him to wish death upon Ray, Dan and Dick simply because of their far-fetched connection with the happening—it's preposterous, insane!"

"It is the way of India," explained Mahatma, "when an offense is considered unforgivable. All must pay. The Taharans were brought to India by Dick Sahib and his friends. That is enough."

Dick, trying to appear composed, leaned back in his chair.

"Doesn't look like our discussion is accomplishing much, does it?" he asked, and forced a smile.

Ray, white-lipped, exchanged glances with her father. Rex Carter, in turn, glanced to Professor Oakwood for some reassuring word.

"I have heard of curses," said Dick's father, gravely, "but have never before had a first hand experience with them. You all recall, I believe, the famous curse reported of King Tut's tomb in Egypt. Anyone disturbing the remains or relics by excavation was supposed to be under penalty of death and several tragedies actually occurred. Some scientists ascribed these fatalities to coincidence but others, more familiar with occult practices, saw evidence of a sinister power at work."

The Professor paused as though loathe to continue, permitting the little group to draw their own conclusions. But Ray, determined to face the issue squarely, requested an exact appraisal of the situation.

"Please don't try to soften the real facts," she urged of Professor Oakwood. "Mahatma doesn't offer much hope. Do you feel that there is something in this curse business?  Is it possible for any human to simply utter words into the air, 'within a week from this day one of you will be dead' and have this thing actually happen?"

"Science has never accepted such a possibility," answered Professor Oakwood.  "There are many things that science cannot understand; we have gradually explained much magic which mystified the uninitiated, and we shall probably reveal, as time goes on, much more apparent phenomena that has the world puzzled at present.  There is usually a perfectly simple, physical explanation to it all once it is discovered.  And, unless this priest assigns someone to do the killings, there is every likelihood, it seems to me, that no harm will befall any of you."

"But, Dad," protested Dick.  "We none of us can afford to wait to see whether this is so or not.  We've got to act, for the time being, as though the curse would work, and do whatever we can to prevent it."

Professor Oakwood nodded, staring thoughtfully at the ceiling.  He had been up against many hazardous and perplexing problems before but this dilemma offered nothing tangible to grapple with.

"I have nothing to suggest at the moment," Dick's father was forced to confess. "I think, however, that I will accompany Rex to the temple tomorrow morning and see if I can add my persuasive powers to his in getting the priest who uttered the curse to change his attitude of mind."

"By all means," urged Rex Carter. "I'll want Dick to go with us, too, in order to identify the rascal."

And so it was arranged.

Mahatma Sikandar was none too anxious to accompany Professor Oakwood and Rex Carter on their mission to the Golden Temple when the following morning arrived. His face bore a hopeless expression and a trace of fear. It seemed that the old crystal gazer was afraid the priest might be further offended and extend his curse to include the whole party.

"But we must risk this," insisted Rex Carter. "You have powers of your own, Mahatma.

Couldn't you counteract the will of the priest somehow?"

The aged Indian raised his hands above his head in a deprecating gesture, as though horrified at the suggestion.

"My powers are not their powers," he said. "To interpose my will would mean death. All any of us can do is throw ourselves upon the priest's mercy."

Approaching the Golden Temple which was again thronged with worshippers, Dick, his father, and Rex Carter fell back to permit Mahatma to lead the way. This the old crystal gazer did with reluctance. Upon entering, the group found themselves in a crowded sanctuary, its floor paved with silver rupees. Half-fed, pinched-faced worshippers were dropping burning camphor-laden leaves into the mouth of a pit. Dick, pressing in, saw these blazing leaves illuminating, far below, the flower-enshrined image of the god Siva. Beggars held out their palms on all sides and Dick found some coins for some of them. But as quickly as he dispatched the coins, more greasy, twitching palms were extended, until he moved uncomfortably away, keeping close to his father and Rex Carter who were having difficulty staying within reach of Mahatma.

"Point out the priest as soon as you sight him," urged Dick's father. "We want to get out of here as quickly as possible."

"I hope," said Dick, rather anxiously, "that I can recognize him. So many of these Indians look alike . . . they're so thin and dried up."

"You can't imagine them having any supernatural power, that's certain," observed Rex Carter. "You wouldn't think they possessed the physical or mental stamina that *we* have."

"Which only indicates the truth, apparently, of that old saying," remarked Professor Oakwood, "that 'appearances are deceiving.'"

It was a curious sight which met their eyes; weary sinners doing penance before a shrine, leaving two *pice*—copper coins—in payment for their sins; sacred monkeys gamboling and chittering about; priests seated like small statues of Buddha, motionless, expressionless, their souls perhaps in Nirvana for the moment. Strange odors offending the nostrils; wisps of smoke, the jumbled mumblings of a multitude at prayer. All of these impressions came to Dick as he searched out the holy man whose curse had placed a limitation upon his earthly life.

"Where is he?" Dick asked himself over and over as he scanned every nook and cranny of the temple.

It was possible, Dick suddenly thought with a feeling of despair, that the priest, if he possessed unusual psychic power, may have known that he was being sought and had removed himself from the scene. Somehow this surmise brought a panicky sensation for Dick had counted, more than he would admit, on the peaceful overtures which he hoped his father and Rex Carter could make. Otherwise, if the priest's invocation of evil was to be taken seriously, a calamitous series of happenings might be expected.

"There he is!" Dick cried out impulsively as he finally glimpsed the object of his search, seated upon folded limbs in the furthest corner of the temple, apparently in deep meditation.

"You sure?" asked Professor Oakwood.

"Certain!" said Dick, recalling the particularly scrawny frame of the ascetic and relieved to find that he could identify him.

"All right, then, Mahatma," directed the Professor. "Will you proceed to the holy man and make intercession for us?"

The aged crystal gazer, his fat figure looking out of place among those of his starved appearing brethren, pushed forward, being closely followed by Professor Oakwood, Rex Carter and Dick. When he came to a spot some several feet in front of the priest, he suddenly prostrated himself, uttering a low moaning sound and making signs with his head and hands. He was using the native tongue and Dick did not know until afterward that he had said:

"Oh, Master, forgive me, a sinner. But I come, bearing offerings from these white brethren, one of whom has incurred thy displeasure."

Mahatma Sikandar then explained the visit of Professor Oakwood and Rex Carter in full, the figure of the priest not revealing by slightest gesture that it had heard what was being said. But, at the finish, with the aged crystal gazer still bending low over his fat stomach, the priest slowly raised his head and opened his eyes. These eyes were directed at Professor Oakwood and Rex Carter and shifted from one to the other, finally coming to rest upon Dick. All three petitioners were made to feel most uneasy by this concentrated attention, particularly since the eyes burned with a quiet condemnation.

"And so, the white Sahib has come to offer up his gold as a sacrifice?" spoke the priest in perfect English.

"I have come to make whatever compensation is within my power for any wrong that has been done," volunteered Rex Carter, earnestly.

The priest gave no answer, his eyes moving weirdly in their sockets.

"We deeply deplore the offense against you and your God," added Professor Oakwood, scarcely knowing how to penetrate the holy man's cold reserve.

"It does not matter," was the low-voiced

answer. "God wipes out all offenses. Time removes all blemishes against the Perfect One. Mere words, Sahib, cannot atone for acts."

"But cannot one act atone for another?" begged Rex Carter. "I am prepared, oh Master, to lay at your feet a fortune in money to aid your poor and destitute worshippers who beg a pittance for bread. I would even endow a great hospital to care for the sick and the blind. India needs many things that wealth could give . . . and if you would have compassion on my son and the members of his party . . . ?"

" 'Vengeance is mine,' sayeth the Lord. Your own Bible teaches you that, Sahib. It teaches also that the only real bread is bread of the Spirit. They who worship here are not poor, they are not starving, their souls are fed and nourished by the inner light of Siva in whom is the love and life everlasting. You in America erect hospitals, treating the effects and not the causes. You worship money as God. But money avails you nothing here, Sahib. You pay and get paid in India for your *deeds*."

Professor Oakwood and Rex Carter consulted one another concernedly. It was turning out as Mahatma Sikandar had predicted; the holy man was adamant, as imperturbable and unchangeable as the image of the god Siva.

"Your God is just," appealed Dick. "He knows that my friends and I were not responsible for the defiling of your temple by my two slave men from the land of the Taharans. Kurt and Kurul, in their ignorance, knew no better. They will learn through many lives . . . but is it just to punish them . . . punish us? Can we not be forgiven . . . can we not repent and be granted a chance to atone through *doing* . . . and not through death?"

The holy man, gazing intently at Dick as he presented his plea, showed not the slightest sign of compassion in his face. A sacred monkey, chattering with almost fiendish glee, suddenly scrambled across and leaped upon the priest's shrunken shoulders. It was as though this monkey knew that the killing of his fellow creature was to be avenged and the manner in which its gimlet eyes blinked at Dick caused a wave of nausea and faintness to pass over him.

This was all so ghastly, so fantastic, so unbelievable. And yet it was turning out exactly as Mahatma Sikandar had predicted. Dick could recall the old crystal gazer's words: "I see a priest talking to Dick Sahib. . . . He points to his sacred monkey . . . and what he says makes you feel . . . what shall I say? . . . sick and faint in the stomach! . . ."

The priest, fondling the sacred monkey tenderly, seemed irritated that the little group of supplicants for his mercy still remained before him.

"Mahatma," appealed Rex Carter, sensing that the interview was about to be cut short without anything having been accomplished. "Can't you address this priest in his own tongue and make him understand our good will . . . our desire to make amends . . .?"

But the old crystal gazer who had wandered from the Way through a pandering to such elemental desires as physical comfort and an abundance of good food, could only shake his head. With such psychic powers as the over-fat Mahatma did possess, he could sense the uselessness of pleading further.

"If we say more," replied Mahatma, "the time of the curse may be foreshortened. The Master is already much displeased. He is asking the sacred monkey whether it desires the blood of the white fathers also."

Professor Oakwood and Rex Carter paled. The priest had been conversing in low tones with the animal on his shoulder, and now, pointing to the sacred monkey, his black eyes burning until they took on the lustre of a red coal, he said: "Your presence, Sahibs, is an abomination in the sight of this holy creature. The god Siva bids me be tolerant else I should pronounce a curse upon all who dare question the justness of eternal wisdom. You will leave this worshipful place at once. I again have spoken!"

With a dismissing wave of the hand, the priest closed his eyes as though to shut out the world and its imperfections. There was nothing for the little group to do but take its departure. And as they pushed their way through the swarm of worshippers, a feeling of despair gripped them. The demeanor of the priest, his unswerving determination to exact the curse, and his seeming confidence that the gods would answer his invocation, had impressed Professor Oakwood and Rex Carter. They were dealing with a power which was horrifying in its possibilities and probably mathematically certain in its working out. The pronouncement of the curse had not just been an idle threat, and the priest's refusal to consider their pleas made it seem as though they had just been turned back by the court of last appeal.

"What can we do now?" Dick asked, as they reached the door of the Golden Temple. "What's our next step?"

His father shook his head, perplexedly. "There appears to be no next step," he said. "I feel, at the moment, as though I were standing on the bottom step with an absolutely black void below and about me. But things have looked black for us all before and we mustn't give up hope. Despite the conviction this priest has, it is still hard for me to believe that any man can wish disaster upon another. So keep your chin up, boy!"

Dick forced a smile. His father had taught

him to face the facts at all times and he was amused now that his parent should be trying to soften the situation by reassurance.

"Don't worry about my chin," said Dick. "I've already taken some real wallops on it and I haven't been knocked out yet."

Rex Carter, worried about his son and daughter, turned anxiously to Dick.

"Have you any idea who the curse is directed at first?" he asked.

"Not the slightest," Dick replied. "That means we'll have to develop the best possible safeguards for everyone concerned . . . and trust to fate!"

This remark drew a disapproving grunt from a dispirited Mahatma Sikandar.

"Dick Sahib cannot trust to fate," he reminded. "For Fate has been ordered against you!"

"Then," replied Dick, with sudden resolution. "I'll have to abide by what happens. If there's any rhyme or reason in this universe—nothing actually happens by accident. Some people are killed by automobiles, others by insect bites and others by disease. There are countless different causes, and what I've seen and gone through has made me something of a fatalist. If, as young as I am, it's written in the sands that it's my time to go, nothing can stop it. Even if I could break the curse, something else would get me. . . . So I'm going to keep as calm and collected about the future as I can . . . at the same time fighting this thing with all the resources at my disposal!"

"You certainly are taking a finer stand about it than I'd be capable of," complimented Rex Carter. "You really feel that way?"

"I do!" declared Dick, earnestly.

As he spoke, a beggar stepped into his path, palm upheld, beseeching a coin. Dick tried to sidestep but the man still blocked him, making mute appeal. A something in the man's face caught and excited Dick's sympathy. He thrust his hand in his pocket and pulled out several rupees.

"Never mind it!" urged Professor Oakwood, taking Dick's arm. "You'd have to give to millions if you once start in."

"No," said Dick, "I just give to those who . . . I can't explain, Dad . . . there's a difference . . ." With that he dropped the coins in the upturned palm.

"Bless you, Sahib!" murmured the beggar, bowing his head. "May the darkness lift from your pathway!"

"What's that?" cried Dick, recoiling in shocked amazement. "Did you hear what this man said?" he asked of Professor Oakwood and Rex Carter who had stopped and were eyeing the Hindu curiously.

The beggar had spoken in softly intoned English. He was a small man, lean of figure, garbed in a loin cloth and ragged sheet which, however, had been washed spotlessly clean, no doubt from submersion in old Mother Gunga.

"What do you know about the darkness of my pathway?" Dick demanded, eagerly.

The eyes of the beggar seemed to light up as he answered with quiet impressiveness.

"I see, Sahib, like images reflected in a pool, that great dangers lie ahead. You have *given* to me, a beggar, and you may now *receive.* Hear then the message I bear for the white boy in quest of true knowledge . . . !"

Dick stiffened with anticipation. He could hear his father and Rex Carter stifle gasps. Mahatma Sikandar had clasped his hands against his stomach and was staring, almost as awed as the others in the party.

"What is the message?" begged Dick.

"A great and holy One awaits you in the mountains of Kashmir," said the beggar. "He alone has the power to help you. Sahib should lose no time making a pilgrimage to him."

"But who is he and where will I find him?" persisted Dick, greatly moved by this astounding information.

"His name I am permitted to give you," answered the beggar, making a worshipful sign. "It is Bhagavan Vamadeva. Sahib had best commit it to memory."

"Bhagavan Vamadeva," repeated Dick. "Will you please write it down, Dad?"

Professor Oakwood took out pencil and notepad. Mahatma Sikandar bowed low before the beggar, recognizing in him a highly developed soul who had elected to mingle with the multitude in expiation of certain sins of the flesh or to perform some designated mission. One could never divine the exact purpose which prompted Hindus who possessed a consciousness of the "inner light" to choose this lowly form of servitude and one could never distinguish them from the common run of low caste beggars unless they cared to reveal themselves.

"I have his name now," said Dick, turning back to the apparent beggar. "But you have not told me where in the mountains of Kashmir I should find the Master!"

"And that I cannot tell," replied the humble Hindu. "No one knows except that he leads those who are deserving to him. I am permitted to say that you are to proceed at once to Srinagar where you will again be directed."

"Srinagar," said Dick. "I have heard of this city before. Isn't it the capital and largest city in Kashmir?"

"Yes, Sahib," declared the spiritual informant. "It lies in the valley, in the shadow of the snowy peaks, below the abode of the Master."

"If you have any way of communicating with Bhagavan Vamadeva, tell him I will commence my pilgrimage to him at once," decided Dick, after a consulting glance with his father.

The supposed beggar nodded. "There are others in your party who will go with you," he stated, as Dick looked his surprise. "Their number is four. They are not to see the Master but it is written that they are to start the journey. Does Sahib understand?"

"I do," said Dick, thinking of Ray and Dan, and Kurt and Kurul. "And may I ask, will they, too, be safe from these dangers which you have seen ahead?"

"I can say no more," was the answer.

Rex Carter, who had stood by, spellbound, now fumbled for his wallet and took out gold pieces which he pressed into the Hindu's hand.

"A thousand thanks for your kindness to us," said the millionaire backer of Professor Oakwood's expedition. "A moment ago we felt beaten, hopeless . . . but now our strength is renewed."

"I am pleased," replied he who was disguised as a beggar, "but keep your gold, Sahib. I have no need for it. A pittance supplies me. What I have told you could not be bought; you had earned the right to know or I could not have spoken."

Rex Carter took back his gold pieces a bit nonplussed that this man who had asked for alms should now spurn a comparative fortune. Mahatma Sikandar, who had used his powers of crystal gazing and other psychic ability without exercising too much discretion in the matter of material things, evidenced humiliation in the presence of the beggar. He who was on the path to true mastership did not sell his spiritual wares in the market place. This beggar, in his self-denying attitude, was reflecting the spirit of the secret brotherhood.

"We can never express our appreciation," said Dick, all but overwhelmed with a feeling of gratitude. "This message may be the means of saving our lives."

"You will persevere, Sahib. The Way is rough that leads to Bhagavan Vamadeva . . . but it is the only way to your salvation."

So saying the apparent beggar raised his arm and took what seemed to be a step backward. Perhaps he merely blended with the natives who were massed about; or perhaps there was some other, more profound explanation for his almost instant disappearance.

"Good heavens!" exclaimed Professor Oakwood, rubbing his eyes. "That man! Where did he go to?"

"It's incredible!" gasped Rex Carter. "I've lost track of him completely!"

"He vanished practically before our eyes!" cried Dick. "How amazing!" Turning to Mahatma Sikandar who stood as though transfixed, in an attitude of great reverence, an excited Dick demanded: "Tell us, Mahatma, were we *seeing* things or did this man actually dematerialize himself?"

"He is gone," was all that the old crystal gazer would say, but his eyes were turned upward to the sky and he was intoning something in Hindustani which sounded strangely like a penitent's prayer.

"It's quite inexplicable!" was Professor Oakwood's conclusion.

"At last!" said Dick, overjoyed, "I've seen a demonstration of occult phenomena with my own eyes. I have had evidence that true masters do exist . . . and a Way has been pointed that may lead to our being freed from the curse. We must get back to the hotel at once and advise Ray and Dan. Not a minute must be lost!"

"No, indeed!" seconded an anxious Rex Carter. "This revelation could not have come by accident. You must go where the finger of destiny seems to beckon. It appears to be your only hope."

"I'm sure of that," Dick replied. "A higher power is about to intervene in our behalf if we can measure up to what is required by that power. Apparently I am the only one who is to see the Master, if he can be reached, but there must be a good reason why Ray and Dan are to start the journey with me. I have faith that we will all be protected."

"That is asking a lot," was Professor Oakwood's comment. "I don't know that my faith is that strong but I do agree that you should search out the Master, as instructed. It is plain that there is no power here capable of dealing with the situation."

With hopes strongly rekindled, the little group hurried back to their hotel.

# CHAPTER V

# IN QUEST OF THE MASTER

RAY and Dan were anxiously awaiting the return of Professor Oakwood, Rex Carter and Dick and knowledge of the outcome of their petition to the priest. When the trio finally appeared there were looks on their faces which were instantly misinterpreted.

"Good boy, Dick!" congratulated Dan, "so you got the old geezer to call off his curse?"

But Dan's expression of relief vanished when Dick shook his head.

"No such luck," he replied. "That priest is determined to make his curse stick."

"Then why aren't you worried?" demanded Dan, looking from one to the other.

"Because," spoke up Rex Carter. "Dick was given a very hopeful message by a beggar. He is to go at once in search of a certain Master . . . the name escaped me . . . ! It's *Bhaga* something . . ."

"I have it here," supplied Professor Oakwood, referring to his notepad. "It's a good thing we took it down."

"Never mind, Dad," smiled Dick. "I know it. The name's Bhagavan Vamadeva."

"Sounds interesting," said Ray, eagerly. "But what can this man possibly do for us? What connection does this have to the curse?"

"I don't know," answered Dick, "except that we were told to lose no time in locating this Master and that we might expect help from him in the danger we are facing."

"Fine!" exclaimed Dan, with enthusiasm. "Where is this bird? How can we get to him—by plane, auto, train, camel, foot or how?"

"That's hard to say at present," declared Dick. "I'd have to consult a map first. We're supposed to head for Srinagar . . . and after that, we're to receive more detailed advice . . ."

"My, so it's *that* mysterious!" breathed Ray.

"Apparently," Dick conceded, "we're told only what we need to know for now. The question is—how soon will you two be ready to start?"

Ray gazed inquiringly at her father.

"Don't you think we'd better accompany you?" Rex Carter asked, turning to Dick.

"Yes," urged Professor Oakwood. "Any venture as important and as shrouded in uncertainty should compel us to keep together for the protection of all."

But in this, Dick did not agree. "You remember, father, the Hindu said there would be four in the party. I am sure he was referring to the four others who had come under the curse. And, somehow, I feel you and Mr. Carter can be of greater service to us here. I'd like to have you keep an eye on this priest. We might want you to act on some communication that we would get through to you. Besides, I don't have any apprehension for Ray, Dan or myself on the trip . . . except as that curse might figure in . . . and I've enough faith to believe, if we reach the Master in time . . ."

"And if you don't?" hazarded Rex Carter, concernedly.

"Well," said Dick, drawing in a deep breath. "We'll just have to cross that bridge when we come to it."

"I don't like bridges," dissented Dan. "I hope we don't have to cross any."

Dick, getting out an aerial map of India, examined it carefully. Perhaps no more picturesque country existed in the world, with its awe-inspiring contrasts of climate and topography. The famous "Roof of the World," the Himalayan mountains with their eternal snows, shut off India from Tibet; to the north and west were the slopes of the highlands of Afghanistan and Baluchistan; extending down from these were the great river plains; next the vast tableland known as the Deccan with the giant stepping stones, the Ghats, sloping down to the eastern and western coasts. As Dick spread out his map, all crowded about to see him trace the distance from Benares to Srinagar with his finger.

"Looks like we're a good eight hundred to a thousand miles away," said Dick, after careful scrutiny. "I don't know whether we can reach there direct by train and I'm afraid we'd arrive too late if we could. If this curse means anything, something's going to happen within this first week."

"You mean you'd like to go by plane?" asked his father.

"I would," said Dick. "Those pilots you've hired have been loafing about here, drawing their pay and no work. I'd fly the plane myself except that I presume it's safer since we have two men specially qualified for the job."

Professor Oakwood exchanged glances with Rex Carter who nodded approvingly.

"I see no reason why they shouldn't go by plane. It appears to be a long, arduous trip any other way and—as Dick points out—every minute actually counts!"

Once decided upon, arrangements were quickly completed. The pilots were notified and went to the field ahead of the party to get the plane in readiness.

"What are you going to do about Mahatma?" asked Dan as he and Dick were feverishly at work packing the things they were to take with them. "Going to leave old Crystal Ball behind?"

"Funny you should ask me that," said Dick. "I've just been turning Mahatma over in my mind, wondering whether it wouldn't be wise to have him along. If we only understood Hindustani it would be different but there might be times when his presence would be invaluable."

"That's what I've been thinking," agreed Dan. "Ever since Mahatma came through on those predictions, I've had more respect for him. I'd have him wrap up his crystal ball and come with us if I were you. We're going into a strange country, mingling with strange people, and I want to know what it's all about."

Dick nodded, hesitatingly. "There's only one thing—that beggar who gave me the message said that there would be four in the party . . . and Mahatma would make five. Do you think, for some reason, we were only intended to take four?"

Dan scratched his head in perplexity. His was not the temperament to solve weighty problems.

"I think it's all a matter of interpretation," was Dan's conclusion. "The beggar probably was referring to the four under the curse and, if he was, I figure we can take Mahatma or anyone else, just as we like."

"All right," accepted Dick, grinning, "then Mahatma goes with us. I'll tell him to pack his nightshirt."

On gaining admittance to the old crystal gazer's room, however, Dick found him in a strangely sober and meditative mood. The crystal lay upon its thin cushion of black silk, giving evidence that he had but recently been gazing into it. And before Dick could make known his desire, Mahatma raised a pudgy hand.

"You are about to ask me, Dick Sahib, a difficult question," he said. "I have just been given a glimpse into the future. I have seen myself on the white-winged bird of the air . . . and I have seen it falling to earth."

Color left Dick's face. Dan who had stepped in the door behind him, felt his pulse beat unevenly.

"Then what would you advise us to do?" asked Dan, after a moment of quite terrible silence. "Should we make the trip by boat and by motor car, even though it is much slower?"

Mahatma Sikandar shook his head, solemnly.

"Some sort of disaster awaits, no matter how Dick Sahib shall go,'" was his reply.

"You don't mean you see any of us getting killed?" persisted Dick as Dan clutched his arm.

"No," said Mahatma. "I see accident . . . delay . . . trouble. I do not see all. We each have a different karma; what happens to you cannot happen to me."

"Then you will not go with us?" assumed Dick, determined not to lose courage.

"I have not said that," replied Mahatma. "One cannot run away from destiny any more than one can escape a curse. It is written that I shall go."

"That's the stuff!" cried Dan, slapping the old crystal gazer on the back. "You're a great scout, Mahatma, if I do say so myself!"

"Dan Sahib will please refrain from such unchaste conduct hereafter," reproved Mahatma, rubbing the shoulder. "I can feel your thoughts; I do not need to feel your hand."

"Okay," laughed Dan. "But that's a regular custom in America when we want to express our admiration for someone."

"American customs," said Mahatma, with a measure of scorn, "are very disturbing."

On returning to their own room, Dick talked pointedly to Dan.

"Listen, old timer. We don't breathe a word about this prediction to anyone else— get me?"

"Don't you think we'd better speak to the pilots?" asked Dan, a bit uncertainly. "Something might be wrong with the plane that they've overlooked which might save us from whatever's going to happen."

"I don't think so," said Dick. "My guess is, if we hinted to the pilots that things might go wrong, they'd never make the flight. Even white men are superstitious, particularly air pilots. Lots of 'em carry good luck charms. I'm not even going to let them know we're supposed to be under a curse. It's dangerous business, Dan. And we don't want your sister to be any more upset than she is, either. So, give me your word you won't spill anything?"

"Just so I don't have to promise not to spill soup," agreed Dan, eyes twinkling.

"I couldn't ever keep a promise like that."

Dick punched his chum, playfully.

"Hey!" mocked Dan. "Kindly cut the comedy hereafter, won't you? You hit me then right in the middle of my concentration!"

Kurt and Kurul, who had been sulking about the hotel, were delighted at the news they were to take to the air again, thinking that this implied a return to their beloved country of Tahara. But the two loyal subjects of Dick Oakwood, king of the Taharans, were disappointed, even terrified at the word that they were to be carried further into unknown country.

"No good!" Kurt kept repeating, shaking his head from side to side. "No good!"

Kurul also registered his protest and it was several minutes before Dick could reassure them.

"Peculiar," he confided to Dan. "They don't know anything about this curse but they act as if they feared something on this trip . . . as though they had an instinctive feeling of danger . . ."

"They sure do," observed Dan. "I haven't known them to fear anything physical, either. Of course they've been scared at things they haven't understood but those two Taharans can be counted on, ordinarily, to fight anything . . . that is—anything except the . . . er . . . *supernatural!*"

"Careful of those big words!" warned Dick, amused. "You're liable to choke on 'em one of these days."

"Say," retorted Dan, "it takes a lot of syllables to begin to express what's been happening to us lately! My head's been whirling like a merry-go-round!"

"Well, don't let it spin too fast," advised Dick, "because something tells me we're going to need all the wits we've got before we're through . . ."

"If you don't let me eat too much I'll be okay," volunteered Dan. "I never can think on a full stomach!"

Professor Oakwood and Rex Carter accompanied their young people to the flying field to bid them adieu. Both men were intensely serious, realizing that much depended on the success of this latest adventure. They did not express what each no doubt felt, that there was a possibility Ray, Dan, Dick or all three might not be seen alive again. The two pilots, crack American aviators, seemed to welcome taking to the air once more, unaware that this trip was fraught with possible great hazard for those upon whom a curse had been pronounced.

"We'll notify you when we reach Srinagar," Dick told his father as he climbed in the cabin plane, after helping Ray up the steps ahead of him.

"Wish you were going," called Ray to her father. "I'm sure we're going to see many interesting sights. India's such an amazing country!"

"Never mind the sights just now!" urged Rex Carter. "Just take care of yourselves!"

A British aviator who had accompanied the party to the plane to see the take-off, offered a comment.

"Here's hoping you reach Kashmir ahead of the monsoon," he said.

"What's a monsoon?" asked Dan.

"The rainy season," informed the aviator. "It's about due to set in. And you never saw such rain in any other part of the world. You people in the United States have an average rainfall of fifty inches a year while some sections of India have between fifty and sixty *feet!*"

"Whew!" gasped Dan. "Maybe we should be making this trip in a boat instead of a plane."

"If you beat the storms you are all right," smiled the aviator. "But there's a chance of your running into the southwest monsoon. Better watch out for it and if you see her coming, pick a soft landing. Cheerio!"

With a wave of the hand, the British aviator stepped back as the tri-motors of the cabin plane hummed into a roar. Kurt and Kurul, seated just ahead of Dick who had taken his seat beside Ray while Dan sat across the aisle with Mahatma, looked out the window apprehensively. This man-made monster which flung itself into space still struck fear in otherwise stalwart Taharan hearts. They controlled themselves quite well when actually in flight but this moment of leaving the earth saw them clinging wide-eyed to their seat.

"Big bird good," Dick said to them as he had said on several former occasions but Kurt and Kurul only clung the tighter.

And the next instant the plane started moving across the field, with Ray, Dan and Dick waving farewell to the figures of their fathers who stood side by side. These figures were soon left in the distance and the ground commenced dropping away so that the spires that dotted the waterfront of the river Ganges glistened in the afternoon sun, further and further below. Circling the field once, the pilots gave their party a second and last glimpse of Professor Oakwood and Rex Carter, two tiny dots that would not ordinarily have been discernable had one not known exactly where to look. Then the instruments were set to mark out a definite course toward the far-away city of Srinagar and the fantastic city of Benares faded rapidly from sight.

No attempt was to be made to make Srinagar in one hop, the immediate destination being Delhi, capital of India, about midway between, where the intention was to spend the night. And those on board settled back to enjoy the ever-changing panorama of the trip, forgetting for the time the threat of danger which was supposed to be hanging over their heads.

It was near sundown when the assistant pilot of the plane pointed out the nearing city of Delhi, distinguished by its famous tower known as the Kutb Minar, whose shaft-like, vari-colored structure could be seen while yet the plane was miles away. Delhi's "perfect tower" stood amidst a vast pile of ruins, some ten dusty miles outside the city, the ruins indicative of the ancient glory which had been Delhi's in the time when it was India's largest city. Built by the followers of Allah, the many-tinted sandstone sides reflecting shadings of purplish reds from pink to orange in the topmost of its five balconies, gave to the architectural wonder a majesty and magnificence seldom equalled as an air spectacle. That the breathless party might better observe it, the pilots obligingly circled the tower which soared to a height of two hundred thirty-eight feet. A throng of admirers scattered below, evidently fearful that the plane was about to make a forced landing but the large tri-motor pointed its nose again into the sky and roared away toward the capital city of Delhi which, in itself, provided an eye-filling sight. About a mile from the town, the plane passed over the historic Ridge—a rocky height of some sixty feet which was the British base during the siege of Delhi after it had been captured by the mutineers in 1857. Dick, vaguely familiar with Indian history, called attention to certain landmarks which even he could recognize. A severe contrast was apparent at their altitude between the native quarter and the British section of the city. Well-kept roads, shady lanes and spacious areas inclosing comfortable bungalows marked the British colony, with European hotels and handsome new government buildings for good measure. But the native quarter looked shabby, squat-like and congested with narrow, crooked streets.

"I've picked my hotel!" cried Dan. "Boy, it looks like we'd be putting up in a real bed for tonight . . . and maybe we'll get cooking that can be translated into English!"

"There you go again!" grinned Dick. "Comfort before everything!"

"Might as well eat, drink and be happy," was Dan's guarded reply, "for tomorrow we . . . !"

Dick stopped him with a warning glance as Ray, touching Dick's arm, gave the word that they were about to cut off the motors for a landing.

# CHAPTER VI

## UNEXPECTED HAZARD

A NIGHT spent in Delhi refreshed the whole party despite their being required to turn out the next morning at six o'clock for a resumption of the flight. Nothing untoward happened which was also encouraging since Dick and Dan had been disposed to look over their shoulders at mere shadows. But the city of Delhi, in the little they had seen of it, had proven so interesting that they had resolved to return for a longer visit, *if* and *when* they were able to lift the curse and its constant menace.

Kurt and Kurul had been unusually self-contained and for this Dick was thankful. He felt a bit sorry for his two loyal Taharans and their obvious cases of homesickness. Thus far he had lacked the opportunity to contrast them vividly with the lowly natives of India, except to make the observation that, however ignorant the low caste Hindu, he was apparently some hundreds of years further advanced than the Stone Age Taharans.

"For as old a civilization as the Hindus are supposed to be," Dick reflected, "the mass of their people are not very highly developed. On the other hand, a few of their race seem to have reached a knowledge of life and a control of the life forces which no other humans have attained. So how can you figure such a contradictory state of affairs?"

Apparently more learned ones than Dick had asked the same question and found it unanswerable. The Hindus, of course, would explain it all on the basis of reincarnation . . . and say that souls climbed the ladder of karma slowly. At this rate, the poor Taharans would have to be born back into the earth life some thousands of times. It seemed like a tedious, discouraging process but the Hindus did not appear to mind it. They possessed almost infinite patience. If a thing was not accomplished in this life, it would be the next, so why worry?

"But this present life of mine is too interesting!" Dick reflected to himself. "And I certainly hope it's not cut short by those few words that a priest spoke into thin air!"

The weather was exceedingly hot and great clouds of dust arose behind the plane as it took off. Dan, remembering the warning of the British aviator to look out for the "monsoon," scanned the distant horizon anxiously. But all he saw was a slight haze, possibly caused by the heat.

Soon the plane was passing over the rich plains region known as the Punjab or "Land of the Five Rivers." This tract of land, about two thousand miles long and from two hundred to four hundred miles broad, without a stone and scarcely a pebble, was composed of river sand and silt washed down through countless ages from the slopes of the mountain walls on the north. The fields below presented a cultivated appearance, tribute to the stolid industry of the peasants. Occasionally a magnificent estate stretched out below and Dick imagined it to be the dwelling place of a Maharaja, ruler of the country.

"I understand these rulers still have harems," said Dick to Dan. "Places where they keep their women from the sight of other men."

"That's a kindness if the women aren't good-looking," Dan observed, dryly, "but it's a crime if the women are beautiful!"

He glanced sidewise at his sister, Ray, who made an impish face at him.

"How about it, Ray?" kidded Dan. "How'd you like to be the wife of a Raja? Pretty swell, huh?"

"Not for me," smiled Ray. "I want to be the only woman in some man's life . . . not one of many!"

Dan nodded as though the subject were one to be taken seriously.

"Hello!" he suddenly pretended to discover. "What you blushing about, Dick?"

Dick had appeared a bit self-conscious and Dan's joshing did not help the situation. Ray's good-humored brother knew too well that Dick admired his sister greatly and he frankly hoped that the two might pair off some time in the future. They were apparently ideally suited to one another and made a stunning looking couple, Dick with his tall, athletic physique, fair hair and blue eyes; Ray with her well-formed body, black curly hair and keen dark eyes. But neither Dick nor Ray had intimated any regard for each other except that of chums on a great adventure, despite Dick's rescue of Ray from several hazardous situations. And now both sought to change the subject which a teasing Dan had tricked that he might enjoy their embarrassment.

"How long do you suppose it will take us to get to Srinagar?" Ray asked.

"Five hours as the crow flies!" grinned Dan. "But that's something I forgot to ask—any crows in this country?"

"Search me," said Dick.

"No use," Dan jollied. "I know you don't have any crows on you."

"You're feeling too good today," was Dick's rejoinder.

Dan, of course, wouldn't admit it, but he was actually nervous. He kidded when he felt this way in an attempt to cover up but Dick was on to him. Dan knew, without saying so, what Dick had in the background of his mind. It was the same thing that had been troubling him . . . Mahatma's vision in the crystal ball of the plane falling to earth before it should reach Srinagar!

Both chums became silent and listened to the hum of the three motors, seeking to detect the slightest indication of anything wrong. But the engines were singing beautifully, a rhythm of motion, the three propellers revolving as one. Dan turned to gaze at the quiet old crystal gazer beside him.

"How you feeling, Mahatma?" he asked.

Mahatma Sikandar looked straight ahead, his eyes concentrated upon the horizon.

"I feel fine," he said, without changing the focus of his eyes. "And you, Dan Sahib?"

"I feel good if *you* do," was Dan's reply, intimating that should Mahatma not be worrying, he saw no reason to be concerned.

But almost as he spoke, the plump fingers of the Indian seer pressed into his arm.

"Can Dan Sahib tell me what he sees afar off?"

Dan strained his eyes.

"Pretty hazy today, Mahatma. Looks like dust."

"Dust!" repeated the old crystal gazer, his body stiffening. "Has Dan Sahib ever been in a dust storm?"

"No," said Dan, face sobering. "Not in this country. But dust doesn't amount to much."

"It is too hot. Something is coming," announced Mahatma, commencing to squirm in his seat. "It is as I feared . . . something is coming."

"What?" reacted Dan, trying to keep his heart from quickening its beat. "I didn't think you really feared anything, Mahatma. I thought you took things as they . . . as they came!"

"Something is coming!" repeated the fat Hindu, gripping the back of the seat ahead. "One meets Fate better on the ground than in the air. Cannot your pilots be made to land?"

"You don't think it's serious?" queried Dan, scanning the horizon again and seeing nothing to be alarmed about.

"Soon it will be too late!" said Mahatma.

Dan immediately leaned over and attracted Dick's attention.

"Hey, Dick! Walk back here with me a second, will you?"

He indicated the rear of the cabin. Dick slid from his seat, wonderingly, Ray looking after him, as the two boys went back for a conference.

"Mahatma's getting uneasy about something," Dan confided. "He thinks we're going to run into something . . . and keeps looking off toward those dust clouds. Do you observe anything to get excited over?"

Dan pointed in the direction they were going. Dick, picking up some binoculars, adjusted them on the horizon.

"I'll say I see something!" he reported, and handed Dan the glasses.

"Whew!" whistled Dan. "Boy, I never saw blacker clouds! They look like a tidal wave. I can see 'em now with the naked eye. They're rolling up behind that dust screen . . . and it's all moving this way mighty fast!"

"Our pilots see it," said Dick, as the assistant pilot glanced back, saw that they were aware of what was coming, and waved his hand reassuringly. "See—they're going to try to go around the disturbance. Let's go back and sit down before we get Ray upset . . . and Kurt and Kurul."

"But do you think we're safe?" asked Dan. "Mahatma thinks we ought to lose no time— that we should land at once!"

"That's because he's not very used to air travel," replied Dick. "We're all right, Dan. This whole storm may miss us. If it doesn't, we've plenty of time to . . . !"

But even Dick, as versed as he was in flying conditions, had no realization of how speedily a storm could come upon one in India. The landscape commenced to darken suddenly, causing a blistering sun to disappear from view. A dead calm prevailed as the plane changed its course but this new direction availed it little.

"Weather bad!" announced Kurt, after a startled conversation with Kurul.

He pointed ahead and then looked questioningly at Dick. What was going to be done about it? Could this big white monster fly through storm and wind? Master Dick should know. He himself had talked to the birds and flown them. Kurt and Kurul had seen this with their own eyes. In moments of peril they had faith that their ruler would see them safely through. But what could he do against the gods of the sky—the thunder and lightning? . . . An ugly flash illumined the way ahead and an angry, billowy mountain of black seemed to rise up to the front and on both sides, choking off escape. The pilots now were looking for a spot to make an emergency landing but darkness had descended and was closing in behind them so that turning back was even out of the question. Lights were snapped on in the plane and Ray's white face looked appealingly at Dick and Dan. Mahatma sat motionless, except for his lips which were moving inaudibly. Kurt and Kurul had expressions of panic in their faces.

"What do?" asked Kurul, wild-eyed. "What do?"

"Sit still!" ordered Dick. "Everything's all right. Sit still!"

But everything *wasn't* all right . . . or no-where near it! A terrific wind now hit the plane which had been flying high, the pilots having striven for a higher altitude in the hope of getting above the oncoming storm.

"The monsoon!" gasped Dan, hanging to his seat to keep from being pitched into the aisle. "It's the monsoon that's upon us! . . . Good grief! Hear it rain, will you? It's just like we're in a submarine!"

Such a deluge of water as Dan nor Dick had ever experienced in the air, now not only descended but seemed to envelop them. Life-giving rain for India, brought in by the southwest wind, was a life-threatening wind for those caught in the sky. The deluge was a mighty cloudburst with a blinding succession of lightning flashes that seemed to sear through the plane. Dick put an arm about Ray to shield her as best he could. Water began to sputter and splash through the air-tight windows. The roar of the storm smothered the roar of the engines but Dick could tell that the large cabin plane was losing altitude. It was being buffeted about by the wind and rain like an eggshell and the pilots were doing a remarkable job keeping it right side up at all.

Suddenly, with a cry of terror, Kurt leaped

from his seat and lunged toward the door.

"Stop him!" cried Dick to Dan, as both tried to follow.

But the plane gave a lurch which threw them into the aisle and a fear maddened Kurt, reaching the door, tore at the handle, throwing his powerful body against it.

"Me go!" he was shrieking. "Me go!"

Kurul, stampeded by the actions of his fellow Taharan, attempted to follow. But Dan grappled with him as Dick fought his way after Kurt. "No, Kurt! NO!" he shouted.

But his Taharan bodyguard, with herculean strength, managed to push the door open. Wind and rain rushed in, snapping the door off its hinges and hurling it into black space. And through the aperture, the form of a crazed Kurt went hurtling.

"He's gone!" sobbed Dick, as his frenzied effort to clutch Kurt almost resulted in his being sucked after.

"It's the curse!" Dan was moaning, as he struggled with Kurul. "Help me hold this fellow, Dick! Help!"

There was nothing that Ray could do but

remain where she was, holding grimly to her seat and praying that all might be delivered from this most terrible of situations. But the open door added further to the plane's instability. And as Dick added his strength to Dan's in an attempt to subdue the ill-fated Taharan, a more startling happening seemed to seal the doom of all on board. . . .

A stab of lightning exploded inside the plane, putting the three motors out of commission and tearing off a section of the wing. Kurul, Dan and Dick were stunned momentarily. Ray, as the plane commenced falling out of control, grabbed at Dick who had fallen half over her seat. Mahatma Sikandar, the whites of his eyes showing, did not budge. Ahead of him two pilots sat at the controls, shocked into insensibility.

"Dick!" Ray cried. "You've got to get to the controls! We're lost if you can't . . .!"

Dick, recovering his senses, lurched over the form of Dan on the floor of the plane and half fell, half dragged himself into the closed cockpit where he reached over the unconscious figure of the pilot and pulled at the controls.

There was a moment of terrible uncertainty as Dick waited for them to respond, fearing that they were entirely out of commission. But the plane suddenly spun about and partially righted itself, its dizzy downward descent somewhat checked. The darkness was lifting as the plane dived toward the ground, lifting enough so that Dick could make out objects indistinctly through the sheets of rain. He worked madly at the controls, noting the damaged wing and trying to place as little strain on it as possible. It was difficult to operate the controls without actually being in the pilot's seat and Dick held his breath as he attempted to flatten the plane off, turning up its nose just as it was nearing the earth.

"Look out!" shrieked Ray.

A large group of buildings suddenly loomed up in front. Dick, struggling to make a dead stick landing, managed to clear the houses on what appeared to be a large estate, and in the next instant the plane struck on one wheel, careened, wabbled to the other side, caught its damaged wing in the ground . . . and turned over!

# Chapter VII

## STRANGE DISAPPEARANCE

FEAR of fire is always uppermost when a plane crashes but Dick had thrown the switch so that the danger of the gasoline's igniting had been diminished. But the crash of the plane was violent enough to rend and tear it badly, shaking the occupants up and hurling them in a heap against the forward compartment.

Dick found himself jammed between the bodies of the two unconscious pilots whom he thought may have been electrocuted from the lightning bolt which had struck the plane. Disentangling himself as quickly as possible, Dick forced his way into the passenger cabin where he found Ray, a gash on her head, sobbing hysterically as she pulled at Dan who was caught under a seat with Kurul on top of him. Mahatma Sikandar was dragging his fat self out from under a pile of wreckage apparently none the worse for wear. But the one desire of all was to escape from the plane

122

before anything worse should happen. Gasoline could burn despite the heavy rain if the tank should explode.

"Help me, Dick!" Ray begged. "I don't know how badly Dan's hurt. He's . . . !"

"I'm okay!" came a muffled voice. "If you'll just get the freight off me!"

Kurul, to Dick's relief, began to come around. Dick gave him a lift and looked about for some means of exit. He sighted a shattered window and pointed to it. A terrified Kurul understood and crawled painfully toward the opening. His head bore a large bruise.

"Go out!" Dick directed as Kurul glanced back.

Rain was pouring in as the lone Taharan, moaning piteously, forced himself through and out into the storm. Excited voices could now be heard outside and a hammering occurred on the plane's side. The voices spoke Hindu and Dick called to Mahatma for a translation.

"They want to know if you are alive or dead," said the old crystal gazer with a faint smile. "What shall I tell them?"

"Tell them we can't decide yet," answered

Dan, who had just been liberated. "Boy, what an experience! I thought we were goners sure that time! Say, Ray, your head's bleeding, did you know it? . . . Here, let me give you a boost out of this dang mess!"

Dan grasped his sister and pushed her toward the window. A Hindu hand and arm reached in and took Ray's wrists. She was lifted through.

"Go on out," ordered Dick of Dan. "I'm going to get the pilots!"

"But you can't get 'em alone," said Dan. "I'll help!"

Together the two chums worked their way forward, clearing such wreckage as they could. The assistant pilot was showing signs of life as Dick reached him. Opening his eyes, the aviator gasped and made a lunge for the controls.

"It's all right," Dick assured him. "We're down!"

The assistant pilot stared wildly about.

"Crashed, eh? What's happened to Jim?"

"You were both shocked by lightning," Dick replied. "He seems to be snapping out of it, too."

With the assistant pilot able to help himself, Dick and Dan dragged the pilot from his seat and managed to get him back to the window which had been cut away by rescuers from without. The pilot was passed up and out; then the assistant pilot followed and after him came Mahatma Sikandar who had been studying the opening with misgivings.

"Mahatma cannot dematerialize," he said. "If I had been a pound heavier, I should have been in what you American Sahibs would call an embarrassing situation. No?"

The old crystal gazer's sense of humor at this rather desperate moment served as a slight relief to the tension.

"After this you'd better go on a diet," advised Dan, putting his shoulder under Mahatma and assisting those on the outside to hoist him through.

"You're next," said Dick.

"No, you!" urged Dan. "You look sick, old boy. You must have been hurt, too!"

"Get on out of here!" spoke Dick, sharply. "I'm last to leave this ship!"

Dan knew better than to argue. Dick had a way of taking charge during emergencies.

"Okay!" he said, and chuckled. "I'm no lightweight, either. Those babies on the outside are sure getting some exercise!"

Holding up his hands, Dan permitted himself to be hauled through the hole. Dick, with a last glimpse around, picked up what luggage he could get his hands on and tossed it up. Then, beseeched by Ray and Dan to abandon the plane, Dick pulled himself out, being aided by willing hands of Hindu servants who were drenched to the skin, as were all of the little party rescued.

It was not until then that Dick revealed his own injury, a badly wrenched knee. He had forced himself to use it during the excitement but now it was all he could do to walk.

"You will come with us to the house," one of the rescuers was saying in Hindustani which Mahatma translated. "Our Chief, Maharaja Zakar Singh is away, but in his name we bid the unfortunates welcome!"

"Holy smoke!" exclaimed Dan. "What a spot we picked to crash! The home of a Raja! Lead me to it!"

The two pilots, still dazed from their experience, were assisted into a magnificent dwelling. Behind them came Dick, leaning heavily upon Dan, with Ray walking on his other side, bowing her head into the wind and rain. Kurul, following along, cried out his grief at the loss of Kurt. Mahatma Sikandar brought up the rear, his clothes looking transparent so closely did the wet garments cling to him. And not one was sorry to have found shelter so speedily, nor to have injuries and comfort administered to.

"Where are we?" asked Dick, when his knee had been bandaged and he was seated in dry apparel furnished him by the Raja's tailor.

Ray had also been given fresh clothes, a loose-flowing dress of the richest oriental weaving which gave to her an entrancing appearance.

"You look like the queen of the harem!" teased Dan.

"Please!" begged Ray, blushing. "They might not like such remarks!" Then, looking down at herself, she said in a low voice. "But isn't this material exquisite? It must be very costly."

"It looks wonderful on you," complimented Dick, quite fascinated by the manner in which the Hindu style of dress brought out Ray's natural beauty.

"You were asking, I believe," said Ray, evasively, "just where we were . . . and I'd like to know that, too."

"I'm afraid," Dick replied, "that we'll have to wait until Mahatma comes in. None of these natives seem to speak English."

In about a half hour the old crystal gazer, himself gayly attired, strode in. The clothes seemed to give him a new sense of importance.

"Hello, Mahatma!" greeted Dan, pretending not to have recognized him at first. "Can you imagine, I mistook you for the Raja. I was just about to give you the royal salaam!"

"Dan Sahib had best not make fun within the sacred walls of the palace," warned Mahatma, guardedly.

"Go easy, Dan," added Dick. "We don't want to get in any more trouble. The fates have been with us, as it is, considering what has happened."

Dan nodded, thoughtfully. "Okay, Dick. I guess I was just feeling relieved at knowing that we've got a couple days' grace before anything else can touch us . . ."

Dick stiffened, questioningly. "I don't get what you're driving at?"

"Well, didn't that priest say in his curse that 'within the first week, one of us would be dead'? If that's true, as we know it was with Kurt losing his life, then it's still several days before the second week arrives when the next death is supposed to take place . . ."

"Dan!" cried Ray, greatly disturbed? "Don't talk that way!"

"I can't help it," Dan apologized. "We've got to think of these things . . . got to do some tall figuring . . . have to face facts . . . you can't tell who it might be next time. And now that our plane is ruined, how are we going to get to Srinagar and find that Master who might save us?"

Dan was asking pertinent questions which did call for an answer. But Dick was provoked at his openly expressed concern.

"I intend to continue my trip to Srinagar tomorrow," he volunteered. "Don't ask me just how yet . . . but I'm going."

"On that game leg?" asked Dan, incredulously.

"I can't let my sprained knee stop me," said

Dick. "I can't let *anything* stop me. The beggar said that I must persevere . . . that the Way to Bhagavan Vamadeva was rough . . . but that it was the only way to our salvation. I believe that thoroughly now."

"So do I!" agreed Ray, tremulously. "These Hindus, many of them, must possess marvelous foresight!"

"*Too* marvelous!" grumbled Dan, ruefully. "And, you notice, none of them see anything good. Mahat looked in his glass ball and saw trouble; the beggar also saw trouble. Personally, I don't want any of 'em to take any more peeps into the future. I can just about see my finish at this moment, myself!"

The three fell into a tense silence, during which they tried to relax by admiring the beautiful interior of the Raja's costly residence. The Indian decorations, furnishings and whole interior must have been worth a fortune. Every effect suggested softness, a quiet blending of color, and solitude.

"Mahatma," addressed Dick, finally. "We have been wondering exactly where we are. Can you tell us?"

The old crystal gazer shook his head. "We're in the Punjab country," he replied, "I understand we're not far from the city of Lahore . . . but I could not say with exactness."

"Next question," spoke up Dan. "How far is Lahore from Srinagar?"

"I think," said Mahatma, looking off into space, "that it is between one hundred and fifty and two hundred miles."

Ray looked disappointed at the distance, glancing concernedly at Dick whom she did not consider in condition to make such a journey.

"Srinagar is in the mountains, isn't it?" she asked. "Close to them, anyway . . . and not so easy to get at."

"I don't know much about it," confessed Dick. "But, hard or easy, I'm going to get through . . . so don't you worry."

The storm which had continued raging, showed no signs of diminution as night came on, the servants extending every hospitality in urging that the party remain until the following morning when the Raja himself was expected back.

"Our Chief will be happy to meet white brothers from the shores of America," one of the servants assured in polite Hindustani. "He will be sorry for the calamitous happening and will help you in your distress."

"That's nice of him," expressed Dick, "but we wouldn't want to impose . . . to outstay our welcome. The Raja's household has already been more than kind."

The servants bowed low as though for their guests to be in distress was to command every attention.

"The first thing in the morning," said Dick to Dan as they were being shown to the room assigned them, "I want to go out in search of Kurt's body. Kurul, poor fellow, is simply beside himself with grief and lonesomeness. I'm going to have him sleep on a rug near us tonight."

"A good idea," approved Dan. "I don't know how you're ever going back to Tahara and explain to your people, as you call them, as to how Kurt met his death. I'm afraid Raal wouldn't understand . . . Kurul might take back the wrong report . . . and the Taharans might rise up against you."

"I've thought of that," admitted Dick, turning to bid Ray good night. "So you're going to be right across this corridor from us?" he observed, with a smile. "Get a good sleep, Ray, if you can. I know it's going to be hard to relax after what's happened today but we need strength for what may be ahead."

Ray gave Dick her hand. "I haven't ever been a burden to you yet, have I?" she asked.

"No," Dick conceded, gazing at her admiringly. "You've made me retract any opinions I've ever had about girls on expeditions . . . and, tonight, well—just take a look at yourself in the mirror, if there is any!"

Ray's face colored prettily. She curtsied and retreated across the corridor as a servant explained through Mahatma that this was the first time a woman had ever been honored by being permitted to remain in other but the fourth deorhi or dwelling place of the Maharanis. Asked what was meant by the Maharanis, the old crystal gazer told Dan and Dick that this meant the Maharaja's ladies.

"But what is the fourth deorhi?" asked Dan, wonderingly.

"It's an inner court," informed Mahatma,

"where no other man but the Maharaja may enter. No male, except a member of the ruling family, may pass beyond the first deorhi, unless he be a doctor or Brahman priest, when he must be heavily veiled, looking neither to the right nor to the left."

"Well, we're learning something anyhow," was Dan's comment, as he waved goodnight to Mahatma.

The two pilots had been ushered to a room further down the long hall, dull red in color. Mahatma was to occupy a room near Dan and Dick. He seemed quite content with his good fortune and quite ready to turn in. The day had been nerve-racking and fatiguing, even for one who practiced a bit of the Yogi.

How long Dick had been asleep he could not guess but he awakened with the premonition that all was not well. Raising up on an elbow and gazing about the dimly lit room, he glanced instinctively upon the floor at the spot where Kurul had stretched himself out. There was a deathly stillness over the place, the rain having ceased and moonlight strayed in the high windows. Dan's face, half in the light, was visible across the way and from the rhythmic rising and falling of his chest, Dick could tell he was dead to the world. But Kurul—where was the surviving member of the Taharans?

"I'll bet he's sneaked out to search for Kurt," decided Dick, and the very thought caused his spine to tingle. "But why didn't Kurul wait until morning? I promised him I'd go with him then. This is ghastly business, going out into this strange country, in pitch black, and alone!"

Dick crawled painfully out of the deep cushioned bed and tested his knee. It was too stiff for him to think of following Kurul as he could not stumble along in the dark. But Dick felt that he had to do something.

"Dan," he said, softly, limping over and shaking his sleeping chum. "Dan, wake up!"

"Oh!" gasped Dan, starting up and gazing about. "Gee! What's wrong? I dreamed I was falling from the plane! Did I holler or something?"

"No," whispered Dick, "but Kurul's gone and I don't know what to do about it. I'd go after him but . . . !"

Dick indicated his injured knee.

"Good grief!" groaned Dan. "Why did you ever bring those Taharans into India? They've gotten us into a peck of trouble and it looks like the one that's left is going to get us into plenty more!"

"I know," Dick admitted, sadly. "But I don't blame them. It was my bonehead. However, we'll have to make the best of it now. I want to do all I can to protect Kurul . . . and get him back to his people safely. If I could turn back now, I'd do it."

Dan put a consoling arm about his chum. "Listen, Dick . . . it's useless for us to chase Kurul at present. We're not in a wild country around here. I doubt if he'll get in any danger. The worst that could happen would be for him to get lost."

"I doubt it," said Dick. "He's got a remarkable sense of direction."

"Then let's wait till morning," counselled Dan, "and try to get some rest regardless. I'm getting over some of this excess worrying. I guess these happenings are making me a fatalist. At any rate, I'm confident there's nothing violent going to happen again until the second week . . . and it probably won't happen then if you can reach that master with the funny name."

"Bhagavan Vamadeva," supplied Dick.

"I'll take your word for it," grinned Dan. "Come on now, Dick! Lie down like a good fellow and don't be so over-conscientious. I've a hunch that Kurul will be okay. Of course I'm not Mahatma, but just you see if my hunch isn't right."

Dick, for the first time, permitted Dan to persuade him. He sank back upon his divan. "All right, Dan, but if your hunch is all wet, I'll never forgive myself . . . or *you* for talking me out of trying to locate . . ."

"I'll take entire responsibility for a change," assumed Dan. "I don't do that very often so you'd better take advantage of it!"

Dick smiled, wearily, and gestured for Dan to return to his own bed. It did seem a bit foolish to become over-excited at Kurul's disappearance. Sleep, however, was out of the question for Dick and he spent the time until the eastern sky commenced to take on a rosy hue, staring up at the high ceiling, reviewing the strange and terrible happenings of the day just past and fearsomely considering the future.

It was then that a sudden commotion outside aroused him to full awareness. A babble of servants' voices in excited Hindustani, uttered in protest against some one or some thing. Sound of a brief scuffle and then a shadow darkening the doorway.

"Kurul!" gasped Dick, sitting up in horror.

Disheveled, wild-eyed, chest heaving from his exertions, the lone Taharan who had acted so proudly as Dick's bodyguard, staggered into the room, bearing a battered form across his broad shoulders.

"I bring Kurt!" sobbed Kurul, laying the broken body upon the bed, a body not only crushed from the fall but clammily moist from the rain and plastered with mud.

Dan, awakened by the outcries, opened his eyes, then shut them again, unbelievingly.

"Kurul," spoke Dick a second time as servants and guards of the Maharaja entered the room angrily. "How did you find Kurt?"

Tapping his forehead, Kurul gave answer in blunt sentences. "Something in here speak to Kurul. The gods take him by the hand and lead him. Kurul is to take Kurt back to his people!"

Dick's blood chilled within him. The distraught, agonized Kurul did not know what he was asking . . . and it would be difficult . . . perhaps impossible to make him understand. Meanwhile, the Raja's servants were getting more and more outraged at the presence of the dead body in the house, placed as it was across the costly robes and fabric of the divan.

A bleary-eyed Mahatma, soft-footing into the room, was pressed into his usual service as a translator.

"They say the Raja will be furious. He will call down the wrath of the god Brahma for this desecration. You must remove and destroy the body at once."

"How do they mean—destroy?" asked Dan.

"They mean to burn," said the old crystal gazer. "And they think it would be well for Kurul, he of the same race, to join his dead comrade on the funeral pyre."

"That's out of the question, of course," said Dick, struggling into his own clothes which were now dry. "Come on, Dan . . . we've got to take a hand here." Then to Kurul who was prepared to give battle. "Listen to me. I, king of Tahara, will protect you. Only do as I say. Carry Kurt outdoors into the morning sun."

"And you will give him life?" begged Kurul eagerly.

"Do as I command!" ordered Dick.

Kurul obediently knelt and lifted the corpse tenderly over his shoulder. The Raja's men fell back as the giant Taharan strode from the room, down the corridor and out of the Palace, followed by Dick who limped after in company with Dan and Mahatma.

"What are you going to do?" Dan whispered.

"I wish I knew," said Dick, fervently.

# CHAPTER VIII

# A FACE FROM THE PAST

To APPEASE a crazed Kurul and, at the same time, pacify an offended Hindu household was not the pleasantest of tasks for one Dick Oakwood to face. He had heard of the famous funeral pyres of the Hindus and of how wives and servants often had sacrificed themselves on the blazing bier of their master, preferring to accompany him to Preta Loka, the world of the departed. The Taharans had observed the custom of human sacrifice on occasion, Dick recalling the narrow escape Ray, Dan and himself had experienced at their hands. But he felt certain that Kurul could not comprehend the demand of these Hindus to destroy the body of the beloved Kurt. The corpse of this loyal Taharan, in Kurul's mind, should be transported back to his people where the proper ceremonies would be performed in committing Kurt's spirit to his gods. Either this, or let Dick Oakwood, king of the Taharans, employ his magic to restore life to one who had served him long and faithfully.

"There, Master!" said Kurul, reverently, as he laid the body upon the ground.

Ray, having heard the disturbance, emerged from the Palace still attired in the garb loaned to her. She was greatly moved when she learned what was happening.

"We'll have to dispose of Kurt's body in some manner," decided Dick as Dan looked on, helplessly. "And we'll have to make Kurul believe it's all right. That's our only way out."

"It's up to you," assented Dan. "You lead and I'll try to give you all the support I can."

Dick, nodding, turned to Mahatma. "Tell the subjects of Raja Zakar Singh that I greatly deplore the sacrilege that has been done and that I will atone by causing this body to be cast into the fire which shall devour it . . . and that I, myself, will offer fit apologies to their Chief upon his return."

The aged crystal gazer, in a tone of distress, communicated with the Hindu servants who bowed gravely and then led the way to a hollow between two hills.

"This is where they wish the cremation," translated Mahatma. "They are willing to help you build the pyre."

"Thank them and tell them that their god Brahma is merciful," said Dick. "I will cause the offending body to be brought to this spot when the funeral pyre is ready."

Kurul, watching these proceedings with a deepening scowl, stood guard over Kurt's shattered body. He was trustful of Dick but apprehensive of these strange dark-skinned natives of India whom he had held in awe ever since his first meeting with Mahatma Sikandar.

"Kurul," addressed Dick, choosing his words carefully. "I have talked to the god Tahara and I am told that Kurt, your brave warrior brother, is needed by his god. I am forbidden to restore him to life."

Kurul set up a wail at this, beseeching Dick to intercede with the gods and get them to grant Kurt his life so that he could keep his comrade company. Dick shook his head, sadly.

"I cannot talk back to the gods," he answered. "They tell me that since Kurt has departed this life in a strange country, his body must be destroyed."

"No, no!" Kurul protested. "We take Kurt back to homeland, Tahara!"

"But you do not understand," persisted Dick. "The gods say that the only way for Kurt to return to his homeland is to burn his body, releasing his spirit. And this must be done within three days after he has died. If a Taharan dies on his home soil, his spirit is free but when he dies in a distant country, it is tied to the body until the body is no more. And these Hindus, our friends, desire to help us. They are willing to build a funeral pyre and to worship the gods with us. Surely my brave and faithful bodyguard, Kurul, will not take a stand against the gods?"

Kurul, surviving Taharan warrior, stood staring at the youth he had recognized as king of his people. The situation was exceedingly difficult for him to comprehend. His faith in the white ruler had carried him safely through many hazardous experiences but Kurul's terrible homesickness, intensified by the loss of Kurt, had tended to make him rebellious. Dick watched the pitiful contorting of his face as Kurul tried to reach a conclusion. He hoped that no forceful measures would have to be employed because, should they be necessary, Dick feared Kurul's mind could not bear up under such treatment.

"I hate to have to do it this way," Dick confided to Dan. "But I know that, unless Kurul accepts this action as ordered by the gods we have no chance of winning his consent. He'll die defending Kurt's body, otherwise. And his opposition may get us all in more trouble!"

"Exactly," agreed Dan. "You're doing the right thing, Dick, even if you are resorting to deception. It's absolutely impossible to take Kurt's body to his country. Besides, these Hindus look like an angry and determined lot! We've got enough of a curse hanging over our heads now!"

Sorrowfully, as Ray, Dan, Dick, Mahatma and Hindu servants looked on, the lone Taharan knelt by the body of his departed fellow warrior. It was a pathetic thing to see the ceremony of grief which Kurul went through. Several times he looked up and glared at those about him as though he felt himself to be among total strangers, without sympathy and without understanding. All watched tensely, anxious to learn what Kurul's decision might be.

Would he consent to Kurt's body being offered up to his god in flames? Or would he prepare to give frenzied battle, compelling those who had developed a fine affection for him to oppose him?

"The gods command," Dick finally ventured, softly, stepping forward and touching Kurul's shoulder as he saw that the Hindu servants were growing restless. "Does Kurul hear the voice of the gods? Does he bow to their will?"

"Kurul bows," came the lone Taharan's answer, his great frame trembling with sobs.

"Then will Kurul bear his fallen comrade to the pyre which has been made ready?" requested Dick, in the same gentle tone of voice.

Obediently, and to the relief of all, Kurul bent forward and lifted the form of Kurt in his strong arms.

"Lead, O Master," he said.

And Dick, motioning to the group of Hindus, took his place at the front of as strange a funeral procession as one could have imagined. The direction was toward the rising sun in contrast to the usual thought of the setting sun in connection with death.

A pyre had been erected in the time that had been given to Kurul's expression of grief and decision to abide by the mandate of the gods. Kurul mounted this roughly constructed pyre and laid the body of Kurt upon it. He then knelt and lifted Kurt's right arm, pointing it toward the sun in a last salute. Tears dimmed the eyes of Ray, Dan and Dick. Even inscrutable Mahatma Sikandar appeared somewhat affected.

"I'm afraid I can't witness this," said Ray tremulously to Dick. "Of course I realize they're not burning anyone alive . . . but to see the body of someone we have known . . . !"

"You'll have to go through with it," Dick advised. "This is supposed to be a high religious ceremony and we must make Kurul feel that all honor is being paid to his comrade."

Ray's lips quivered. "All right," was her reply. "I'll manage somehow . . ."

Mahatma, edging over to Dick, caught his eye and said in a low voice, "These Hindus are very superstitious. They think the presence of one of Taharan blood is an ill omen. They are going to demand that Kurul be made a living sacrifice."

"But I thought living sacrifices were a thing of the past in India," protested Dick.

Mahatma Sikandar stroked his grey beard. "Who can say what is a thing of the past in India?" was his cagy answer. "I have warned Dick Sahib of what is in the minds of these Hindu brothers."

The old crystal gazer indicated an increasing number of the Raja's household and bodyguard. Dick had not imagined there were so many on the estate but more, it seemed, kept arriving, and they now numbered more than a hundred. To attempt to physically resist such a gathering would be madness. The saving of Kurul, if the Hindus demanded his life, would depend entirely upon his wits. And now one of the guards to the Raja's palace, after a consultation with others of his fellows, approached Dick gravely, bowing low and addressing him in Hindustani.

"What does he say?" Dick asked.

"He says," replied the old crystal gazer, "it pains him to announce that the living Taharan must be requested to lie down beside his dead companion and let the flames atone for his offense against the god Brahma."

Dick drew himself up with all the authority he could command. His blue eyes flashed with a pretended indignation as he gave answer.

"Tell them that they have mistaken the will of their god Brahma. He is too merciful a god to require the life of one who is crazed with grief over the loss of a loved comrade. Any sin this Taharan has committed in their eyes is one of ignorance and not of intention. And their god Brahma knows this. If they will consult their god again, they will find it is so."

Mahatma listened intently and turned, addressing the Hindus in their own tongue. The guard retired momentarily for a discussion and then stepped forward once again.

"What does he say this time?" asked Dick, anxiously.

"He says," repeated Mahatma, "that it is not for the white brother to interpret the thought of their god Brahma. The Taharan must surrender his life, either peacefully or forcefully. You are to make this known to him at once."

Dan, who had been taking in the exchange of messages, grabbed Dick's arm.

"Dick, there's a lot of Indian ponies grazing just the other side of this hill. Do you suppose we could make a break for it, jump these ponies and get away?"

"Not with my bum knee," reminded Dick.

"I'd forgotten about that," said Dan, uneasily.

"We couldn't escape that way, anyhow," said Dick. "Even though we're all good riders, we'd be sure to be caught. We've got to stick here and put up a front of some kind. I'm going over to speak to Kurul. You watch Ray."

Dan gestured to his sister to come close to him. Dick with a nod to Mahatma to stand by, strode over to the pyre where Hindus were awaiting his action, ready to put torches to the pile of wood.

"Kurul," spoke Dick, "will you leave Kurt and come to me?"

The lone Taharan straightened, arose from the side of the corpse, gave a last look at the former likeness of Kurt, and stepped down from the pyre.

"Yes, O Master?"

"You have aroused the anger of the Hindu

gods," said Dick, speaking in the Taharan tongue and groping for words to make Kurul understand. "You are in danger, Kurul, and you must do exactly as I say. They wish to burn you along with Kurt. Do you understand?"

Kurul stared hard and then shook his head. "Kurul no understand."

Again Dick explained, stalling for time as much as he dared and trying frenziedly to think of a way out. Firebrands were being lighted and the Raja's guards began closing in. At last Kurul understood; a deep-furrowed scowl creased his forehead. Turning he beheld a torch being applied to the pyre. Flames leaped up and about Kurt's dead body.

"Does the Taharan go willingly?" Mahatma was translating as the Hindu guards made their last demand.

Kurul, himself, gave answer by grabbing a blazing club from the fire and brandishing it over his head. He waved it furiously and uttered the Taharan battle cry. Dick and Dan were quick to follow his example. With Ray shielded behind them, they stood between the blazing pyre and the startled Hindus who, with a contemptuous regard for fire, started moving forward enmasse.

"We're done for!" gasped Dan. "They'll make us all roast. But I couldn't let them fry Kurul."

"Mahatma!" cried Dick. "Intercede if you can! Get them to call a halt. If the Raja were only . . . !"

The shrill note of a bugle rang out!

"It's the Raja now!" breathed Ray, joyously. "See! . . . There he is, riding this way with more of his men!"

"Boy, is *he* just in time!" said Dan, relieved, as the Hindus turned about to greet their lord.

"That all depends," declared Dick, still worried. "If the Raja is too provoked by our being here and what's happened, it may not help us a bit. But I certainly am going to appeal to him for all I'm worth!"

Throwing aside his firebrand and instructing Dan and Kurul to do likewise, Dick prepared to meet his majesty, the Maharaja Zakar Singh, who had just returned from visiting a neighboring province and was greatly perturbed at encountering these strange and unhallowed events upon arriving home.

"What does this mean?" he inquired from leaders of his household, Mahatma translating for Dick.

A black picture was painted by his superstitious followers who pointed to members of the party accusingly.

"Explain that we meant no harm," ordered Dick of Mahatma. "Tell the Maharaja exactly what happened. Appeal to his sense of justice. He has dealt with white people before. He must have learned justice from the British."

Mahatma Sikandar advanced and paid his respects. The Maharaja, in turban and flowing robes, dismounted from his Indian pony and stood with a hand on the flank of the horse, eyeing the old crystal gazer gravely. At the conclusion of Mahatma's petition, the Raja made no comment but stepped forward in the direction of Dan and Dick. As he did so, Ray moved out from behind her brother and the Hindu ruler beheld her for the first time. Attired in the native dress loaned her, Ray made a lovely picture. The Raja stopped and stood regarding her as though spellbound.

"Those eyes," murmured Ray, to Dan. "It seems I've seen them somewhere before."

"Me, too," said Dan, under his breath. "But, of course, I haven't. Most of these Hindus have the darndest eyes, anyhow. They seem to look right through a person!"

"I'm afraid he's angry because I've been given this costume to wear," said Ray, nervously.

The pyre behind them was now a mass of flames and Kurt's body was no longer to be seen. Kurul had fallen to both knees and was gazing into the fire, mournfully. Dan and Dick waited breathlessly as the Raja, finally taking his magnetic eyes off Ray, continued to advance until he stood before them.

"What do the Sahibs have to say?" spoke the Raja in surprisingly clearcut English.

"We salute you, Raja Zakar Singh," responded Dick who always acted as spokesman. "And we express our profound regret to have invited your disfavor and that of your household by our presence and our acts."

The Maharaja remained silent and motionless, his eyes fixed upon an uncomfortable Dan and Dick.

"And we beg the mercy of your god Brahma," Dick continued, concernedly.

"May your god spare this native son of Tahara who meant no offense. His brother Taharan's body has just been fed to the flames
in accordance with the desires of your household. But we beseech you that no living sacrifice be demanded."

After a long moment of consideration, Raja
Singh turned and uttered a command to his
subjects who bowed low in obeisance. Most
of them then backed away, salaaming as they
went, leaving only the personal bodyguard
which had ridden up with their Master.

"The god Brahma has given ear to your
plea," Raja Singh then announced. "The
hand of forgiveness is placed upon your heads.
You will return to the Palace as my guests and
partake of a morning repast before resuming
your journey."

"Our gratitude, O Raja!" spoke Dick,
greatly relieved.

"Yes, much obliged!" added Dan, quite
without formality.

And Ray, feeling that she should also express her appreciation, bowed prettily as she
said: "We thank you for your great kindness
and compassion, O Rajah."

Again Maharaja Zakar Singh's eyes went to Ray, studying her intently.

"It is a privilege and an honor to serve one so fair; one whom the raiment of our native India so becomes," was the gracious response of the Raja.

"There, Sis," whispered Dan to a blushing Ray. "You see, the Raja's not peeved at your wearing the dress of his women . . . I mean, the kind of clothes the women of this country . . . well, you know what I'm driving at."

"Sssh!" warned Ray, afraid that the good will of the Raja might be injured by the wrong comment. And then, in answer to the Raja's compliment, she replied: "I am grateful that your Majesty was not offended to find me so attired."

"Shall we proceed to the Palace?" bowed the Raja, dismissing his pony to the care of a groom who took it over the hill to turn it into pasture with the other horses.

Dick nodded consent and stepped to Kurul's side, tapping him on the shoulder.

"We will go now, with the ruler of the household, to eat at his table," said Dick.

Kurul arose and followed respectfully behind as the group composed of Ray, Dan, Dick, Mahatma and the Raja, with his attendants, walked back to the Palace. As they left the little valley, all looked back for an instant at the smoldering embers of a fire that had devoured the last vestige of Kurt's mortal remains. And each was reminded, solemnly, of the curse and its apparently inexorable fulfillment. No time must be lost in their effort to secure a release from the deadly spell which had been cast over them.

A marvelous morning meal was awaiting the guests of Maharaja Zakar Singh. All were seated at the table but Kurul who was compelled to eat by himself in a secluded spot. The breakfast, as Dan insisted on calling anything he ate before noon, was served in the garden. At this festive board, Dick became on friendlier terms with his hospitable host, the Maharaja, who had caused Ray to be seated on his right in the place of honor. Feeling that the Raja's sympathy had been thoroughly captured, Dick ventured to confide the purpose of his journey.

"A curse," said the Raja, gravely, "if spoken

by a priest can only be broken by a great and holy man. Who is this Master to whom you have been directed?"

"His name," said Dick, "is Bhagavan Vamadeva."

Raja Zakar Singh paused in the process of lifting food to his mouth.

"He is one of the greatest," confirmed the Maharaja. "But I doubt the ability of Oakwood Sahib to find or to see him."

"Why?" asked Dick.

"Because Bhagavan Vamedeva is reported to live by himself in a mountain cave that is most inaccessible. Pilgrims, seeking him, have fallen to their deaths trying to scale the sheer walls and precipices which lead to the Master's abode. Oakwood Sahib could not have intended to expose his white sister to such danger?"

Raja Singh's dark eyes looked with concern upon Ray who toyed nervously with her food.

"I'm used to danger," said Ray, helpfully. "I shouldn't be shown any special consideration just because I am a woman."

"Ah, but you should!" insisted the Maharaja, gently. "We in India protect our women, not only from the sight of men but from the sight of anything unpleasant. We treasure them as the fairest flowers of life. It was never intended that woman's path should be the same as man's. She arrives at the end of the Path by a different road. And it would be madness for Oakwood Sahib to have you accompany him further."

Ray, Dan and Dick looked at one another, greatly upset and perplexed. If the Maharaja spoke the truth, then they faced a most important decision. Obviously Ray could not be expected to undertake anything so hazardous and yet the problem of what to do with her, now that they had come this far, was apparently unsolvable. She might be sent back, by slow stages, to Benares, in the company of the two pilots since the cabin plane could not be salvaged. But neither Dan nor Ray would listen to this suggestion.

"We can't give up; we must go on," stated Ray, determinedly. "It may mean death either way and I'd rather meet it going forward."

"Well spoken," approved Raja Singh, "your

valor is a noble virtue. But it can avail you nothing at the moment. Far better that you should remain here and accept the abundant hospitality this Palace affords, than courting death which even now hangs over you."

"But I . . . we couldn't think of imposing upon you!" gasped Ray, only to add, appreciatively. "Of course we're most grateful for your offer but . . . !"

"Wait a minute, Sis," counselled Dan. "This might not be such a bad idea. If the Raja is willing to keep you here, I'm sure Dad would be glad to reimburse him for whatever expense he's put to . . ."

Raja Zakar Singh raised a hand, his dark eyes flashing.

"No one pays the Maharaja for a deed of human kindness. We are in this world to serve."

"What do *you* think, Dick?" considered Dan.

Dick Oakwood was frankly at sixes and sevens. He had not expected such exceptional treatment, neither had he anticipated that the quest of the Master was going to be fraught with such difficulty.

"I think," said Dick, speaking slowly, "that it might be well for Ray to remain here, if it is acceptable to the Maharaja. His suggestion appears to be a sound one. From the message that I received in Benares, we were all to start the journey and yet I was to be the only one of the party to reach the Master. And that's the way it seems to be working out."

Ray's disappointment showed in her face.

"But, Dick," she appealed. "This makes me feel like I've been a burden."

"On the contrary," Dick reassured, "it may be a part of the plan through which we are all to be saved. I am sure, in the Maharaja's keeping, you would be well protected."

"She would not want for anything, neither would she have cause to fear," smiled Raja Zakar Singh, and turned to a long silent Mahatma to urge: "You tell her, O seer, the regard and respect a Raja has for women."

Mahatma Sikandar pulled at his grey beard.

"No women are treated with more affection," confirmed the old crystal gazer.

"Then you think it would be okay to leave Ray here?" asked Dan.

"You to remain also?" queried Mahatma.

"Why, I—I hadn't figured on . . . no, I was going ahead with Dick," said Dan.

"Dick Sahib and Mahatma had best continue on," declared the Hindu guide and prophet.

"But you're too fat," protested Dan. "You never could climb the side of a mountain."

"Dan Sahib is a lump himself," reminded Mahatma, dryly.

"I get his point," counselled Dick, in a low voice. "He feels it would be safer and better if you stayed as company for Ray . . . while he and I go to Srinagar with Kurul as our bodyguard. I can't really see now what you would be needed for along with me and the smaller the party, the quicker we probably could push on. I'd feel easier if you stayed with Ray, too."

"Well," considered Dan, "of course the food here is simply swell—but if I thought I could be of aid I'd gladly put my appetite behind me."

Dick grinned at the manner in which Dan balanced his appetite against a sense of duty.

"I can give the pilots money enough to take them to the nearest airport and charter a plane back to Benares where they can report to our dads on what has happened thus far. Then I can return here to pick you and Ray up after I have seen the Master."

"You mean—*if* and *when* you have seen the Master," corrected Dan. "We ought to arrange it this way, Dick. If I haven't heard from you inside a week, Ray and I will push on to Srinagar and do what we can to get trace of you."

"Better wait two weeks," suggested Dick.

"In two weeks," reminded Dan, "there may be no use in waiting. If I remember that curse, death is supposed to strike three times the third week. If it does, it cleans us all out and nothing matters. So you'd better do some tall mountain climbing as soon as you get a line where this Master is!"

"Trust me!" said Dick, and looked down testily at his injured knee which he hoped would be able to stand any strain placed upon it.

"Then the Sahibs have decided to listen to the voice of wisdom?" inquired Raja Singh. "And leave the fair one where no harm may befall her?"

"We have," announced Dick.   "And if it is not too much of an imposition, we should like her brother, Dan Sahib, to remain also."

The eyes of the Maharaja seemed to cloud.

"That is not necessary."

"But we would not wish to leave his sister here without another member of our party," Dick explained.   "It is not because we fear any harm . . . it is merely to keep her company so that she will not suffer from loneliness nor homesickness."

"Does a woman who travels in foreign lands get homesick?" asked the Raja, a smile revealing glistening white teeth.

"I could stay here alone as well as not," declared Ray, bravely, "since you seem to think it best.   I wouldn't want to hold Dan here."

"I must insist upon it," replied Dick.   "I wouldn't feel right about leaving you here otherwise."

"If the Sahib insists," accepted Raja Zakar Singh, "but, as I have said, it is not necessary."

And so it was arranged.   But when Dick came to the making of his own plans for continuing the journey, he was again at a loss as to what to do.

"What is the best way to reach Srinagar from here?" he asked of the Raja.

"A railroad would take you part of the way," the Maharaja informed. "But you will have need for ponies sooner or later. May I not supply you with the fleetest ponies from my stables?"

"You are too kind," Dick replied, overwhelmed by the courtesy. "If you would only let us pay you for such services as you are making possible to us."

"Money is not our god," answered Raja Zakar Singh. "What I possess it is a pleasure to give others. You will come with me and select the ponies you desire . . . and such equipment as you will need."

It seemed all too good to be true, the remarkable co-operation which was being given.

"Imagine our falling out of the sky into this!" exclaimed Dan as they stood by the corral and Dick pointed out the ponies he wished. "That guy is a regular Aladdin's lamp! You rub him the right way and he produces anything you want!"

"If we were in America we'd think there was a *catch* in this somewhere," Dick confided. "I still can't say that I like a certain look in the Raja's eyes."

"Why be finicky over his looks?" joshed Dan. "I'm getting accustomed to these Hindu gazes. Way to judge these boys is by how they act, not how they squint at you."

"Maybe you're right," conceded Dick, as the three ponies were caught and saddled. "It sure looks, on the surface, like we've run into a streak of good luck for a change."

"Sure!" encouraged Dan. "We're going to pull out of this on top. I feel like a piker staying here but I can see it's the right thing to do. Give my regards to the Master mind when you meet him, which I'm hoping you do, and tell him I'll try to see him if he ever comes down off his mountain. I like to meet folks on the level."

Dick, swinging himself onto his pony with Dan's aid because of his stiff knee, trotted the horse up and down to try him out.

"Seems good to be in the saddle again," he announced. "And this pony's a peach."

Mahatma Sikandar, after considerable grunting, had gotten astraddle his mount, while Kurul had leaped easily upon the horse delivered to him. Such belongings as they needed were tied on and the Raja, presenting Dick with a pearl-handled revolver, urged him to take it as an extra precaution.

"Goodbye, Ray," said Dick, reaching down to take her hand.

"Goodbye, Dick," Ray replied, her lips quivering.

"Be a good sport about this," Dick urged, giving her hand an extra squeeze.

"I'm trying to," said Ray, "but I can't help feeling uneasy . . . about you."

"You mustn't worry," comforted Dick. "We've all gone through many threatening experiences together and we're still living. I'll reach this Master if it's humanly possible . . . you can depend on that."

"I know," replied Ray, looking up at Dick, admiringly, and seemingly reluctant to release his hand. "We'll be waiting for you here. Please get word through to us as soon as you can."

"I will," promised Dick, and pulled his pony about to motion to Mahatma Sikandar who was engaged in Hindustanic conversation with the Maharaja. "Are you ready?" Dick called.

"Ready, Dick Sahib!" answered the old crystal gazer who looked a bit grotesque astride the sturdy pony with his over-sized paunch.

"So long, Dan!" cried Dick. "Don't over-eat! I'll be seeing you!"

"You'd better, old pal!" was Dan's rejoinder as he gripped Dick's hand, running along beside the pony. "I'll take care of things here. Those aviators will be on their way back within an hour. Chances are that Dad will want to buy another plane when he finds ours has been destroyed. Good luck!"

"I've got to have it!" said Dick, grimly. He pulled rein beside the Raja who was afoot. "I can never thank you enough for all you have done," he told the Indian ruler. "But I hope some day to show my real appreciation."

"It is nothing," was the Maharaja's answer, with a dismissing wave of the hand. "May I send with you an escort?"

"No, thanks," rejoined Dick.

"I have already instructed Mahatma Sikandar as to the shortest route," informed the Raja. "May success be with you!"

With a farewell gesture, Dick beckoned Kurul to give spur to his pony as he, with Mahatma, rode from the Maharaja's estate, headed toward distant Srinagar.

Ray stood upon a little rise of ground with Dan beside her, his arm reassuringly about her, both watching the three riders until the horizon line dropped them from sight.

"Well," said Dick, in an attempt at lightness. "It looks like it's the dividing of the way!"

And Ray, on the verge of answering, glanced about to find the Maharaja regarding her with a strangely possessive gleam in his eyes. She shrank back, awesomely, and pinched Dan's arm as she gasped: "Now I know! Those eyes I told you I'd seen somewhere before. They're the same eyes of that Hindu who stared at me from the balcony across the street, our first night in Benares!"

"They *can't* be!" mumbled Dan, startled. "You're just imagining things, Ray! ... It—it's impossible!"

But the arm about her tightened protectingly.

"I—I'm sure of it!" Ray whispered, frightenedly. "I can't tell you *how*—but I'm *sure!*"

# CHAPTER IX

## HIDDEN PERIL

WITH the rainy season to contend with, the fair weather which had greeted Dick on the resumption of his journey in quest of Bhagavan Vamadeva did not remain long. Clouds began rolling up by late afternoon with lightning flashes chasing across the sky. Dick, knowing how quickly torrents of rain began falling after a sign appeared in the heavens, commenced looking for a shelter. They had traveled sometimes upon regular highways, again along narrow paths, through an entrancingly beautiful country that seemed to grow in natural beauty as the trio pressed further and further toward the famous valley of Kashmir. In this region, despite its periodic visitation by thunder, earthquake, avalanches and floods, the climate and the surroundings had every appearance of an earthly paradise. Even Mahatma Sikandar forgot the discomfort of jouncing up and down in the saddle to wax eloquent about the scenery in this part of India. Years ago he had invaded Srinagar with a camel train and remembered the mountain peak known as Nanga Parbat, its mighty snow promontory reaching to an austere height of twenty-six thousand, six hundred and twenty feet! Nanga Parbat, home of the eternal snows, with life and warmth and green things nestling at her feet like fertile footstools! Dick could hardly wait to see the outline of this majestic mountain in the distant haze—a sight which would signal that the end of his journey was near. But, at the moment, shelter from a second storm was urgent. This he sought beneath a great overhanging rock, the back of which was turned against the oncoming wind and rain. Tethering the ponies so that they, too, would be protected, Dick spread some blankets on the ground and motioned to Kurul and Mahatma to make themselves comfortable.

"We may have to spend the night here," he said. "It looks frightfully black."

"The blackness may pass as quickly as it comes," observed the old crystal gazer. "Then again it may linger for hours. Even I cannot predict India's weather!"

Dick, looking off in the direction from which they had come, suddenly detected four figures on horseback who appeared to be urging their steeds toward another spot that might serve as a haven from the storm.

"Funny!" cried Dick, studying the travellers intently. "From here it looks like their ponies came from the same stable as ours."

Mahatma grunted and shrugged his shoulders.

"All Indian ponies look alike, Dick Sahib."

"I don't know," rejoined Dick, not so certain. "Do you suppose, by any chance, Raja Singh has ordered some of his riders to follow us at a distance and see that we come to no harm?"

The old crystal gazer shook his head, plump fingers scratching amusedly at his beard.

"Dick Sahib refused an escort. The Maharaja is too much a respecter of wishes to go against your will."

"I suppose you are right," decided Dick, and turned away as the four horsemen were lost to view behind a clump of trees which were bending low in the gale.

Wind, rain and lightning came like an

avalanche shortly after, such a tempest as to make the ponies whimper with fright. But, dry and safe as Kurul, Mahatma and he were beneath the rock, Dick watched the cloudburst with thrilled interest.

"When it rains in India, it means business, doesn't it?" he grinned.

Kurul, who had been used to great storms in the land of Tahara had still never experienced such downpours. Besides, this storm depressed him terribly for it was not unlike the one which had resulted in Kurt's death . . . and he sat moodily staring into the darkened landscape.

"I guess we're stuck here for the night," decided Dick, finally, as there seemed no abatement. "I hope this doesn't continue for several days or we'll have to swim to Srinagar."

"It may continue for a week," said Mahatma whose own spirit seemed to have been dampened. "This country is not new to floods. Sometimes the heavens wash the valleys clean of crops and men. The rivers of earth cannot hold the rivers from the sky and God's wrath extends over many miles . . ."

Dick, confronted with the possibility of be-

Raja should request me not to put on my own clothes again?" queried Ray. "They were dried out this noon and while I'll confess they can't match these I have on, still I didn't dress for beauty on this trip!"

"It's probably just a whim of the Raja's," said Dan, lightly. "Or maybe it's a custom. You certainly look better in those togs so why not keep 'em on till we get ready to leave? Won't hurt you any."

"But I don't like the way he looks at me," protested Ray. "Haven't you noticed?"

"Listen, Sis, you're getting too sensitive for words!" rejoined Dan. "Cut it out. We've got enough to worry about as it is."

How long Maharaja Zakar Singh had been standing behind them, neither knew, but it was Ray who suddenly felt a premonition of someone's presence and turned her head, catching sight of him smiling down upon her.

"You will pardon me, my fair one," greeted the Raja as Dan stared in surprise. "But I have come to escort you to your place of retirement."

Dan gave Ray a quick glance as much as to say, "I told you so." These Indian customs were funny things, silly to Americans but very serious to them. They had a proper place for everything and a caste system where one in a lower grouping of society or humanity didn't mingle with a higher. There was much paying of respects, bowings and scrapings, the grand oriental manner. But it all conveyed a very definite, interesting, colorful atmosphere and Dan, having slowly acclimated himself, was commencing to enjoy it . . . and be amused by it.

"Well, Sis, it looks like you're going to be given a swell boudoir tonight," he joked in a low voice. "That's what you get for being a woman. I have to sleep on a couch or funny divan. Okay, of course, but if the moving pictures are correct, you'll have a private swimming pool and everything. Pretty soft!"

Ray gave Dan a warning nudge. She was perfectly satisfied with the room to which she had been assigned. It was not intended for a woman's occupancy but it would serve nicely, particularly since it was just across the corridor from the room where Dick and Dan had been.

"Must I . . . I mean—do I have to change?" she asked, a bit upset and not wishing to offend this offer of hospitality. "You've already put yourself out so much for us that I . . ."

"The innermost realms of the Palace are open to the fair ones," was the soft answer of the Maharaja. "If you will accompany me to the second deorhi or portal, where maid servants are waiting to welcome you, they shall show you to your private abode in the Inner Palace which shall be yours so long as you remain."

Ray looked inquiringly at Dan, uncertain as to whether to accept or how to diplomatically refuse.

"Go ahead," urged Dan, guardedly. "You're being paid a great compliment. I'll bet it's one of the first times a white woman has ever had a chance to see a Raja's Inner Palace. You'll have plenty to tell about."

Ray hesitated, and hoped while she did it, that Raja Singh might interpret this as shyness rather than an unwillingness to comply. Apparently Dan felt no apprehension whatsoever and considered the opportunity presented her as a great adventure. But Ray had not been able to get over her first impression of the Raja nor her uncanny feeling that he was one and the same man who had all but hypnotized her with those eyes as he stood on that balcony in Benares. It was ridiculous to feel this way, of course, for there were millions of people in India, many who looked strikingly alike, and such happenstances didn't occur in real life.

"If your majesty wishes it," Ray finally acquiesced, "I shall be glad to accept the hospitality, though it is quite unnecessary for my comfort."

"Ah, but it is!" insisted the Raja, pleasantly. "A fair one is made happy by maids who may administer to her every want. These ministrations are not possible in the Outer Palace . . . but where you shall be taken . . ." Cutting off his thought, Maharaja Zakar Singh gestured toward Dan as though to hurry Ray's departure. "You will wish to bid your brother good night, will you not?"

"To be sure," said Ray, and leaned forward to kiss Dan on the cheek. "Dan, I'm sort of frightened," she managed to whisper.

"Night, Sis," grinned Dan, squeezing her hand. "It's all right," he reassured. "I wish I was in your shoes!" And then, as Ray gave him a reproving glance, he added: "Aw, you know what I mean. Don't ever try to tell me a girl doesn't get the breaks! ... See you in the morning!"

Ray nodded and permitted the Maharaja to take her arm. She could feel his cool fingers against her bare flesh and they seemed to chill her. Dan followed the two to the large open court which separated the first deorhi from the second. A military guard stood at the door and stepped aside to permit the Raja and his white lady to pass, but quietly and effectively blocked Dan's way.

"I wasn't going any further anyhow," he said to the guards, amiably, and watched his sister until she was lost to sight across the court, attendants holding a canopy over her head to keep off the driving rain. "Great place," was Dan's comment as he turned back, conscious that he was sleepy and ready for bed himself.

Ray's timidity grew as she was escorted further and further from Dan, past the guards who stood stiffly at the entrance to the second deorhi where two meek maid servants awaited her arrival, bowed humbly before their Master and fell in behind, with discreetly appraising glances at Ray.

"How far are we going?" asked Ray as the Raja smilingly led her through a winding, dim-lit corridor, dull red in color, with a strong scent of otto of roses.

"Be patient, fair one," was his only answer.

Another deorhi or portal was reached where more maid servants joined the party and Ray, now wide-eyed at the magnificence of her surroundings and the secret atmosphere of the Inner Palace, uttered a half protest at going through the fourth and last deorhi which formed the entrance to the home of the Maharanis or mistresses of the Maharaja.

"Ah—but here is where a place has been prepared for you," said the Raja, softly, and with a graceful gesture toward the innermost realm of the Palace which was lost to mankind—a domain that he alone, of the males in the household, had the privilege of entering. On rare instances a doctor or Brahman priest had been admitted but only after being heavily veiled that their eyes might not behold the ladies of the Inner Palace.

"It is all very beautiful," Ray felt impelled to say as she found herself in a house of spacious rooms, richly ornamented with perfumed silks and muslins, the warmest and thickest of carpetings, and latticed windows opening out onto gay verandas, themselves walled in by courts which screened the ladies of the Maharaja from the outside world.

"Your soul will languish here in happiness," spoke the Raja, much pleased at Ray's expression of pleasure at the surroundings. "And now," he said, taking her hand and bowing over it. "I shall leave you in the custody of the Khwases or maids-of-honour. May your sleep be dreamless and you awaken to a new day of delight." With this pretty speech, the lips of the Raja touched the top of Ray's hand.

"Thank you for your many kindnesses," Ray forced herself to say, still too awed at what was happening to be sure just how she should react.

"Trisa speaks English," informed Raja Zakar Singh, nodding to the maid-of-honour who seemed to be in charge. "Make known your desires to her."

Without giving Ray an opportunity to say more, the ruler of the Palace did an about-face and strode from the Inner Residence.

Despite the rain and the wind which continued into the night about the shelter that Dick had selected, he had managed to doze off. Kurul, insisting on affording what protection he could, had lain on the outer side. Mahatma, however, had preferred to lean up against the inner wall of the cliff, drawing a blanket about his corpulent form.

"I would much prefer sitting than lying," he had said to Dick.

"Apparently that's what most Hindus do," was Dick's comment. "Although I'll bet you can't double your legs up under you."

Mahatma had shaken his head, sadly. "Exercise, Dick Sahib, is not a part of my Path of Life. A true Yogi keeps his body and mind nimble. Would that I had done this years ago; but to try it now would break bones and cause much discomfort. The science of crystal gazing is easier!"

Dick had grinned as he stretched himself out to one side of Mahatma, prepared to get what sleep he could even though the morrow might reveal a landscape largely under water. No sense in worrying; he was under enough of a strain anyway. And so, having dropped off to sleep, Dick was dead to the world until he came to with Kurul shaking him by the shoulder.

"Master, O Master!" Kurul was calling in a low, warning voice. "Danger near! . . . Danger!"

Dick sat upright and gazed about him into inky blackness. He was conscious of only the incessant beat of the rain at first, then gradually noticed that the ponies were aroused and alert to some presence which they could sense but not see. Reaching for the pearl-handled revolver that Raja Singh had given him and wishing that he had possessed even more effective firearms, Dick crept to the edge of the overhanging rock and peered out into the darkness.

"What is it?" he asked of Kurul as Mahatma remained huddled, apparently deep in slumber.

"Don't know," answered Kurul, tensely. "But—danger!"

Spat! Spat! Spat!

Bullets! . . . Rifle fire! . . . Bright flashes in the darkness and a stinging sensation in the flesh of Dick's shoulder.

"Down!" he cried, and pulled Kurul to the ground with him.

His quick move was none too soon for other shots whizzed over their heads, chipping off pieces of rock behind. And Mahatma Sikandar, aroused at last, still kept his composure by remaining as stationary as he had when imperilled by the falling plane. Dick, however, answered the shots by firing back, pointing his revolver at the flashes. The ponies, frightened by the firing, tugged at their tethers, ready to stampede. And then, almost as soon as the fusillade had burst forth, there was naught but the sound of horses' hoofs galloping off, splashing through water and striking unevenly against rises of ground!

"It's those men I saw following us when the storm hit!" cried Dick, excitedly, turning toward Mahatma. "It must be! I don't think anyone else could have gotten near us in this storm or known where we were! . . . But what do you suppose their object was?"

"Robbery, perhaps!" said Mahatma, straightening up.

"Robbery?" considered Dick. "But they didn't have to make an attempt on our lives!"

He felt the flesh wound in his shoulder, realizing that it still might be hazardous to use a flashlight or strike a match. "You all right, Kurul?"

"Kurul hurt," reported the lone Taharan, holding up his hand.

Dick could barely see the arm but by feeling the injured member he could detect that a bullet had passed through between the bones.

"Not bad," he said, relieved, then looked toward Mahatma as he asked: "I don't suppose you were hit?"

"My life is charmed," chuckled Mahatma, showing remarkable composure. "I am too easy a target—good marksmen scorn to shoot at me."

"We'll have to take great care after this," said Dick, seriously. "It seems hard to believe that attack was from a bandit band. It's strange that I should get the feeling yesterday afternoon those horsemen were members of the Raja's forces!"

"Dick Sahib is most imaginative at times," returned Mahatma. "Why should the Raja or his men bear you malice?"

"That's what stumps me," Dick admitted.

"Unless," he added, speculatively, "there should be some reason why the Raja should not wish me to reach Bhagavan Vamadeva!"

"Then why should the Maharaja have given Dick Sahib ponies, supplies, a revolver—and his friends the succor of his Palace?" questioned Mahatma. "Dick Sahib cannot be using his reason."

"In India," spoke Dick, deliberately, "I have found that two and two do not always make four. Sometimes too much kindness is evidence of a designing mind. And if that Raja . . . !"

"It grows lighter in the east," observed the old crystal gazer, diverting Dick's thought. "And the rain lifts somewhat. Perhaps, in an hour or two . . ."

"We will push on as soon as it is daylight," Dick declared. "Travel will be slowed up because of the flooded roads and passes. I hope to reach Srinagar within three days at the most."

Mahatma Sikandar moved, stiffly.

"To think that some of my countrymen sit on beds of spikes when a saddle would do just as well," he said, somberly. "You white brothers have far too much physical industry. When you meet Bhagavan Vamadeva he will teach you to sit long in one place—and then you will get as fat as Mahatma!"

But Dick was not in the mood for Hindu jesting. The old crystal gazer's light-hearted reaction to this attempted death-dealing attack was a bit hard to understand. To Dick it almost seemed as though Mahatma had been expecting the onslaught. Come to think of it, he had carefully deposited himself to one side of the cavern-like rock so that he was out of the direct line of fire. Then he had shown no excitement when the shooting had occurred. Whether to put this self-control down to Hindu temperament entirely or whether to be suspicious that the Mahatma was aware in advance of the happening was quite beyond Dick's figuring. But he decided privately to trust none but his own impressions hereafter.

With daylight and the resumption of the journey, Dick's misgivings were further increased on learning from a villager that they were miles off their course toward Srinagar.

"What's the matter with you, Mahatma?" Dick demanded, angrily. "I thought you assured me we were going in the right direction?"

"I cannot understand," was the old crystal gazer's answer. "This man must be mistaken. I would swear . . . !"

Greatly upset, Dick asked native after native, many of whom confessed to having visited Srinagar on missions of worship, and all who could understand his questionnigs, gave the same information.

"Why have you been instructing me wrongly?" Dick asked as Mahatma appeared disturbed. "I have not known you to be deceitful before."

"It was an honest mistake," appealed the old crystal gazer. "I was but following the directions given me by the Maharaja."

Dick eyed the aged Hindu closely. If he were now telling the truth and had not erred himself, then the Raja had wilfully desired that the travelers should miss their goal. And, if this was so, what had been the Raja's motive? What had this ruler of an Indian province to gain?

"How am I to know what to believe?" said Dick. "How can I ever trust you again? You knew that every hour lost might mean the lives of others under this curse! If you knowingly misled us, Mahatma, you are an old scoundrel and I wouldn't hesitate to . . . !" Dick put his hand on his revolver.

"Please, Dick Sahib!" begged Mahatma, putting up a fat hand in protest. "Have I not demonstrated my faithfulness time on time? It grieves me that now you should . . . !"

"I've depended on you," declared Dick, unmoved by Mahatma's sentimental plea. "But I shall do so no longer . . . and should I catch you in another wrong move, it will go hard. This little expedition cannot afford mistakes!"

"I have heard," acknowledged the old crystal gazer, humbly. "I am sorry. It shall not happen again."

And with that, Dick urged his pony in the right direction, bent on making up all the lost ground possible. Kurul followed close beside him, Mahatma bringing up the rear, fingering his gray beard agitatedly.

## Chapter X

## THE LOVE SEEKER

Morning at the Raja's Palace was an awakening in fairyland to Ray Carter who had been put to bed by a retinue of comely Hindu maidens in a room so luxurious as to be breath-taking. She had managed to banish her fears and had sunken into a relaxed slumber which found her refreshed and radiant at the dawning of this new day. Again the rain had vanished with the sun filtering through departing storm clouds and Ray, venturing out on her veranda, inhaled the flower-scented air.

Oh, it was good to be alive! And it was thrilling to be in such a paradise! An experience that she would remember so long as she might live! Dan had been right. This was the thing for her to have done. She had been needlessly foolish in fearing the Raja and his intentions, but not having been accustomed to oriental hospitality it had seemed as though the kindnesses were being overdone.

"Will the fair one have her bath now?" said a soothing voice behind her.

Ray turned to see Trisa with great towels over her arm and powders and perfumes.

"Why—why yes, I would!" she heard herself saying, quite delighted.

"Then the fair one will follow me," said Trisa, whose English seemed every bit as good as Ray's. So saying, she led the way to another door opening off the same veranda, and down a flight of stairs to a brilliantly tiled room with a sunken floor in which reposed a crystal pool.

"Oh, how beautiful! How wonderful!" Ray exclaimed.

"It is for the favored one," smiled Trisa, bowing low.

"The *favored one?*" asked Ray, her face sobering.

"The favored one," Trisa repeated, without explaining. "Now if the fair one will slip off her gown, she will find the water of exactly the right temperature . . ."

Frowning slightly, Ray did as she was bidden and stepped toward the pool, touching the water gingerly with her toes. Ray loved a good swim and the water was most inviting.

These Hindus were always using such exalted terms. Perhaps she shouldn't have questioned being referred to as "the favored one." Raja Singh had called her "the fair one" from the moment he had met her but had apparently meant no more by it than if he had addressed her as "Miss." Well, why worry about it? The idea of having a whole pool for her own enjoyment!

"Here I go!" announced Ray, with a backward glance at the attendant Trisa.

Pushing off with her feet from the side and arching her back, Ray cut the water in a pretty dive, raising hardly a ripple as her body slid down close to the tiled bottom. She came to the surface, tossing her rubber-capped head, and waving at the Hindu maid servant whose eyes gleamed at the swimming prowess which Ray was displaying.

"This is great!" Ray called.

And she swam about, using the American crawl as she stroked from one end to the other, then submerging and going for distances under water, and finally floating leisurely on her back.

"The fair one's breakfast is about to be

served," said Trisa, at length. "She had better dress now."

Ray left the pool reluctantly but wondering a bit why she was not to have breakfast with Dan. Instead, she was told that she was to be honored by the presence of the Raja. What could this mean? More Hindu custom? It required patience to put up with all these funny goings on despite the exquisite treatment. Here was one race, in its higher castes, that apparently took time to extract the fullest joys from living while turning a deaf ear to the world of business.

Dan, on arising, wandered about the Outer Palace, keeping half an eye out for Ray whom he expected to join him momentarily that they might breakfast together. And when time went on without her arrival, Dan approached some of the men servants, demanding to know where she was and when he might expect her. But the servants, who spoke only Hindustani, made helpless motions with their hands and showed their teeth in pleasant smiles.

"Oh, for Mahatma!" groaned Dan. "I sure need a translator. There's a mix-up here somewhere but I can't figure out what it is." Then, turning once more to the servants, he asked: "Where's your Master? The Raja? . . . I want to see the Raja!"

The servants understood this and pointed to the Inner Palace.

"Tell the Raja I want to see him!" Dan insisted.

But again there was the helpless gesture of shoulders and hands. A babble in Hindustani conveyed to Dan Sahib that the Raja could not be disturbed. He was lost to the world when he was in the Inner Palace and all must wait until the Master desired to emerge.

"This is a fine howdy-do!" Dan fumed as he was led to a table in a cozy alcove where an appetizing repast had been laid out for him. "Oh, well—I'll get it straightened out as soon as I see his Nibs, the Raja. . . . Meanwhile, I suppose it's a good idea for me to eat, even if I have to do it alone!"

Ray, meanwhile, having been massaged by Indian maids, perfumed, and attired in the most attractive of morning costumes, had been led into the presence of the Maharaja who sat beside a table richly adorned with steaming food.

As Ray entered with an attendant upon either side, Raja Zakar Singh arose and bowed smilingly in greeting. But Ray stopped short, choking back a startled outcry.

Standing before her was a Hindu in white turban and a blue flowing garment. The one and the same man whose eyes had held her hypnotically entranced that first night in Benares when she had looked out the window of her hotel room and seen him standing across the street in a balcony!

"The fair one will please be seated," invited the Raja, in soft, soothing tones.

Ray felt the hands of her maids-of-honour touching her elbow on either side. Her feet moved forward mechanically, with her eyes never leaving the face of this strange Hindu personage whose gaze again seemed to shatter her own thoughts, to compel her movements.

"The fair one is even more lovely this morning," the Raja was saying as Ray sank into a cushioned chair beside him. She did not reply at once and her admirer took one of her hands, pressing it to his lips.

"Raja Singh!" said Ray, finally finding her voice, at the same time withdrawing her hand from his grasp. "I have seen you before!"

"In Benares!" acknowledged the Maharaja, magnetically. "Our souls communed in one glance. I knew then what destiny had in store for you—that we should meet, as we have, at my Palace!"

Ray could only stare speechlessly at Raja Singh as the slow and terrifying realization began to grow that he had her in his power.

"But how could you have known?" she gasped. "And what could I possibly mean to you?"

"In India," said the Maharaja, his dark eyes looking deep into Ray's, "much is written in the stars. For two years the signs have portended the arrival of a white girl of ravishing beauty who should become my favored one."

"Favored one?" repeated Ray, the true significance of this term dawning upon her. It had not been just a flattering phrase as Trisa had used it. The "favored one" had meant the Raja's favorite wife or Maharani. "But you can't really . . . !" she started to protest.

"A flower comes slowly into full bloom," smiled the Raja, as if to dissuade her fears. "It first must be nourished with loving care and every tenderness in its new environment. You were born to blossom in the heart of my heart. You shall never want for any earthly thing . . ."

"Stop!" cried Ray, pushing back her chair and rising from the table. "Let me out of here. This is impossible . . . outrageous! Where is my brother? . . . Take me to him! I won't stay another minute!"

"You will be seated," said the Raja in even tones, fixing his commanding eyes upon her. "The fair one does not wish to be foolish. She knows inwardly that this is her place, her destiny. Then the sooner she learns not to resist, to let her happiness rest with her Master . . . !"

Raja Singh stepped to her side, touched Ray with his hands and forced her gently back in her chair. Maid servants stood quietly but formidably at every entrance. There was no escape.

"What have you done with my brother?" Ray demanded, panic stricken. "This is fiendish! . . . You will suffer for this, Raja Singh! You can hold me here but I'll never . . ."

"You will have a sip of this wine," urged

the Raja, holding a goblet to her lips. "It will steady the fair one's nerves . . ."

Ray restrained an impulse to knock the glass from his hands but decided that she must use her wits. To put up a fight and create a scene would not result in her release. The Raja was too well fortified, the residence of his ladies was too far removed from the outside world.

Taking a draught of the liquid, Ray was conscious of the sweetly pleasant taste, then of a dreamy dizziness.

"Take the fair one to her room," ordered Raja Singh of the maid servants as Ray slumped unconscious in her chair. "When she awakens, the voice of reason will speak within her. Give her food then, and drink, and tell her that her brother is safe."

So saying, Maharaja left the fourth deorhi, the innermost realm of his Palace, greeting many of his beautiful Maharanis as he passed down the long corridor of luxurious rooms and on into the outer world.

Dan, considerably upset by this time, and having finished his breakfast, was pacing up and down awaiting the appearance of the Maharaja. The moment that the Raja stepped through the portal, with a military guard on either side, Dan accosted him.

"See here!" he demanded. "Where is my sister? I thought I was to see her first thing this morning. If you're up to any funny stuff . . . !"

"Dan Sahib will calm himself," spoke Raja Singh, eyeing him, coldly. "The fair one is quite happy and content to remain, for a time in the Inner Palace."

"I don't believe it!" said Dan, hotly. "I didn't like your looks at the start . . . and now that I see you in that white turban and blue costume . . . you're the same Hindu who . . . !"

"Has no other man of my race ever worn a white turban and a blue robe?" replied Raja Singh.

"There's a look about you!" insisted Dan. "Those eyes! . . . I thought for awhile that most Hindus' eyes were about alike . . . but I know there's a difference now. I can't understand how we ever came to meet again . . . but I know you're holding my sister against her will!"

"There is only one Will," was the Raja's

maddening reply. "Every soul must bow to
the dictates of Karma. Life is so ordered."

"I don't know what you're talking about
but I want you to produce my sister at once!"
declared Dan, defiantly. "If you don't . . . !"

"Dan Sahib is enjoying the freedom of the
outer Palace," was Raja Singh's answer. "His
sister is being suffered no harm. But if Dan
Sahib wishes to preserve his freedom, he will
utter no silly protests."

"Well, this is the darnedest thing I
ever . . . !" sputtered Dan, and then bit his lips.
Perhaps, for the present, he should use discretion. After all, he was one against many.
That his sister was in some sort of peril there
was no doubt. But how to rescue her was a
problem he'd have to figure out. Just now
the whole situation seemed hopeless. What
a fool he had been to encourage Ray's going
with the Raja! He might have known that the
Hindu Master's attentiveness to his sister was
not mere oriental hospitality. And he should
have positively identified that face and eyes,
regardless of the costume Raja Singh was wearing or the place in which he had been met.
Things could happen in India more fantastic

and unbelievable than in any other country in the world . . . and danger threatened in a hundred unseen, unimagined ways!

"All right," surrendered Dan, deciding to bide his time. "You win, Raja."

"Dan Sahib has taken on wisdom," smiled Raja Zakar Singh, and continued on out of the Palace, leaving a sorely perplexed and greatly disturbed young man behind.

It was three torturous days and nights before a worn but determined Dick Oakwood came within sight of the city of Srinagar, basking in the shadows of the great mountain peak, Nanga Parbat, whose snow crowned summit could be seen for miles before the destination was arrived at. Three times the trio of travelers had gotten off the course and been forced to retrace lost ground. And twice it had been a strangely bungling Mahatma Sikandar who had guessed directions wrongly. In addition, his crystal gazing ability seemed to have left him for attempted impressions had failed to work out as he had predicted. Mahatma's only explanation was that perhaps he, too, had fallen under the spell of the curse with wrong information being given to lead Dick astray and result in harm befalling him. Dick, his confidence in Mahatma badly shaken, had listened but had acted on very few of his hunches.

"Now that we're here," he said, wearily, "what happens next? We're supposed to be given further information as to how to reach the Master. I certainly hope we don't have to wait long for it. We're already going into our second week and no telling what that means!"

Mahatma Sikandar pulled thoughtfully at his gray beard.

"I wish, Dick Sahib, that I could help. I should like to meet the Master myself, though I fear I am not worthy. There are lesser wise men here who would be glad to exchange some of their wisdom for my knowledge of the symbols which I memorized from the crown once belonging to the Queen of Sheba. But whether I shall see any of them or not is in the lap of Fate."

"I am interested only in getting to Bhagavan Vamadeva," declared Dick, provoked at Mahatma's expression of his own interests when he knew what a life and death matter the rest of the party faced.

Kurul, in his simple way, had been made to understand the importance of the mission and was eager to be of what help he could. The lone Taharan had overcome his feeling of grief at Kurt's loss and was courageously trying to carry on in the service of his Master, Dick Oakwood, whom he still accepted as king of the Taharans.

Srinagar, capital and largest city of Kashmir, was found by Dick to be a veritable mountain Venice, where the frail tenements of the poor and the elaborately carved villas of the rich huddled along the Jhelum river in neighborly confusion. Seven kadals or bridges spanned this historic river as it passed through Srinagar, a city thronged with all manner of worshippers making pilgrimages to the sacred shrines of the Saints of Kashmir, men who were believed to be in constant communion with the occult world. Mingling with the people, Dick picked up threads of information, his ears and eyes ever on the alert for a message which would lead him straight to Bhagavan Vamadeva. He dared not ask since this would indicate his lack of faith but his patience was being sorely tried as several fruitless days passed without a word.

In this time, Dick heard much of the sacred cave of Amarnath, high up in the mountains and dangerous of access, many pilgrims having lost their lives in trying to reach it. Years ago the Maharaja of the district had refused to cause a path to be built to this cave, declaring that much merit of its attainment would disappear if the Way were made smooth. And so the natives continued to toil up the precipitous slopes, risking life and limb to bow at the feet of the inscrutable holy men who bestowed their blessings upon those hardy enough to reach the hazardous heights.

One of the sights of the city was the faithful carpet weavers who could be seen, bending to their intricate task with a devotion and a zeal that excited as much admiration as their lovely weavings. Dick was moved to stop by one withered looking old woman in whose face burned a flame of unquenchable spirit and whose bony fingers, though shaky, still possessed a nimbleness and deftness of touch.

"Very beautiful!" Dick could not help exclaiming as he gazed down at the pattern on the carpet which he could see reflected the great mountain Nanga Parbat, with some of its passages and crevices outlined in colorful relief.

"You like it, Sahib?" spoke the aged woman, surprising Dick with her knowledge of the English tongue.

"I have never seen anything so perfect!" said Dick, and meant it sincerely.

"No, no!" said the old carpet weaver, making a holy sign. "It is not perfect. No work of man is perfect. See—this much is left undone. We must not finish anything. It is God alone who finishes!"

Dick felt a tremor go through him, a high and fine feeling which seemed to lift him to a new plane of thought. To think that he would encounter such philosophy and such inspiring humility from a mere weaver of carpets!

"I understand," he said, humbly, his eyes suddenly brimming with tears as he reached for some coins in his pocket. "You are deserving of better things, Madam, than such work as this—as wonderful as it is." So saying, Dick dropped some rupees on the carpet.

"No, Sahib!" refused the aged weaver, gathering up the coins and thrusting them back in Dick's hand. "One does not beg who does the Father's work. The pittance for my labors is enough; the rest is love." And then, as their eyes met, the trembling hands of the aged woman suddenly clutched Dick's hand, closing it tight upon the coins as she said: "O, Sahib, it is for you that I have made this carpet!"

"For *me?*" repeated Dick, incredulously.

"See!" cried the old carpet weaver, pointing with a gnarled, bony finger to the pattern of the mountain. "See this secret path! The design was given me by a Master. He caused me to trace out the Way for you to reach his abode. You are to take this, Sahib, as your map and it will lead you to this spot, the unknown cave of the great Bhagavan Vamadeva!"

# Chapter XI

## DIZZY HEIGHTS

So SACRED did Dick consider the revelation made to him in the form of the carpet containing directions for reaching the Master, he said not a word to a curious Mahatma Sikandar except that he could wait no longer and had decided on an exploratory trip into the mountains with the hope of being directed to Bhagavan Vamadeva on the way.

"And you do not wish me to go further with you?" asked the old crystal gazer, a bit crestfallen.

"I do not," said Dick resolutely. "Kurul and I will take our ponies and proceed on by ourselves. When we get to a point in the mountains where the ponies can no longer be used, we will continue our search on foot!"

Mahatma Sikandar nodded, soberly.

"Very well. Dick Sahib probably thinks he knows best . . . but the crystal foretells bad fortune."

"I don't care what the crystal predicts," was Dick's answer. "You've gotten as many wrong impressions as right lately and I refuse to be swayed either way . . . As for you, if you desire to look up other wise men while we're gone, do it by all means. Here is enough money to see you through."

Dick paid the old crystal gazer a goodly amount, sufficient to relieve him of any further feeling of obligation should the paths of the two not cross again. Then, in the company of his dependable Kurul, and guarding carefully his precious carpet, Dick mounted his pony and the two rode off, side by side, through the streets of Srinagar, leaving Mahatma Sikandar, one time wizard of African Jungles, scratching his gray beard and staring hard after them.

Out through the foothills they rode, pilgrims now themselves in quest of a Master who resided some place in the vast mountain which towered above and before them. Ascetics of a sort lined the way, some squatting at every crossroad; funny-looking monks peered out from their monasteries, and keepers of shrines busied about; under fig trees along the ascending path, naked ash-smeared religious men sat, mute signposts to wayfarers, men whose bowls were filled by the poor country folk. It was a changing scene of pain, of poverty, of misery, and of inspiration. Dick, observing all, did not pretend to understand. He could only sympathize and try to appreciate. What was this pearl of great price which even the lowliest peasant was willing to sacrifice life and all material possessions to attain? What did they actually seek in these gruelling pilgrimages, these body-crippling rites which some performed, and the punishing practice of self-denial? Was one glimpse of a holy man and a flash of his transcendent spirituality all-satisfying? Could ills of the flesh actually be cured by a word or a touch from the Master?

"I wonder if I will ever know the answer to any of these questions?" thought Dick as the sure-footed ponies climbed higher and higher on the winding road which led up the ever-steepening side of Nanga Parbat.

There came a time when villages were left behind; when naught remained above but wilderness; when ponies could no longer struggle upward without the risk of tumbling into yawning chasms. It was here that Dick found a sheltered, fertile spot and made the ponies fast with enough rope so that they might graze over quite an area in perfect safety and yet remain within reach for use on the downward trip should Kurul and he return by this route. If not, some other pilgrims must surely come upon the animals and claim them.

Here also the secret path, woven into the carpet, began. And Dick, consulting the unrolled carpet, traced the line up the patterned mountain side. Then, after a half hour search he located the path at the foot of a steep slope. There were niches just wide enough for a footing and crags overhead barely sufficient for a hand hold.

"You go first!" said Kurul. "I follow!"

Dick, interpreting this request as fear on Kurul's part, put aside all supplies and wearing apparel that he could do without and started the ascent with the Taharan following. Dick's knee, fortunately, had grown much stronger since its injury, due largely to his having been able to keep off his feet for some days on the journey to Srinagar.

"Coming all right?" Dick called after they had gone some fifty feet up.

"I come!" was Kurul's reassuring answer below.

Several times, unintentionally, Dick had sent loose stones and dirt hurtling down, some of which had struck Kurul on the head and shoulders. He had been in such a position that he could not look down and the face of the mountain above had seemed to be growing more and more sheer. At times it had been necessary for him to scrape and cut a grip for his fingers with a knife which he carried that had served him on many expeditions. Each hazardous step that he took upward caused Dick to realize more and more the extreme danger he was facing. The mountain abode of Bhagavan Vamadeva was all but inaccessible. The chances were that few, if any disciples had reached this Master. And Dick was thankful now for the cliff-climbing experience he had had in the land of Tahara at the time he was battling and subduing the cliff-dwelling Gorols. But those cliffs were child's play to these monstrous walls. Occasionally, when no indentations existed overhead, Dick was forced to edge precariously sidewise until he found a place to go higher. And, finally, ar-

riving at a narrow shelf where he and Kurul
could pull themselves up and sit a moment in
safety, Dick was staggered by the view.

"Great heavens!" he exclaimed, as a wave of
dizziness and faintness almost overcame him.
"Look, Kurul!   Did you ever see such a sight?
That valley, miles below!   Srinagar off there,
where we came from!   The river Jhelum,
looking like a thin strip of celophane!   Wular
Lake, a great crystal ball!   Mahatma Sikandar
ought to be up here to gaze into it!   What he
might see if he did—the old two-faced rascal! . . . Say, doesn't this make you feel that
Man is an insect? . . . No wonder the Masters
live in high altitudes.   It gives you a feeling of
power . . . as though you'd overcome the
world.   It's a greater feeling than being up in
an airplane because you're still in touch with
Mother Earth . . . and yet in another existence . . . so far removed from everything you
can almost hear your own thoughts!"

Dick glanced sidewise at Kurul after this in-
spired outburst and saw the lone Taharan
grinning at him and shaking his head.   Kurul
hadn't understood much of what had been said
but he had caught the general idea.

The carpet, which had been rolled into a compact bundle and strapped to his back, was undone again that it might be consulted. Dick might have made a copy of the design or outline of the path on a piece of paper but he had been so afraid of missing some important marking in the remarkably woven fabric that he had decided on carrying it with him, despite the extra load it made.

"Well, let's go again," said Dick, after a good rest during which time he had tried to steady his nerves. This looking down had undermined a bit of his courage when he realized what a little slip could mean. And the precipice still stretched threateningly above, as if in defiance of puny man's attempt to scale it. Apparently, however, according to the path shown on the carpet, Kurul and he were almost directly under the Master's abode. All they had to do was continue the climb until they reached a narrow ledge which seemed to be broken with a much wider ledge set back from the face of the cliff.

About two hours of daylight remained and Dick hoped, if possible, to reach the designated spot before sundown. He did not relish the thoughts of perching on a narrow crevice through the night when a slight move in the wrong direction might mean sure death. Far below and off in the distance came a low rumble. Gazing in that direction Dick perceived a great storm moving upon the valley. Black clouds, jagged lightning and wind were sweeping in upon Srinagar while up above, where he was, the mountain side was bathed in the late afternoon sun, distant peaks with their snow caps glistening.

"Nature is certainly awesome!" breathed Dick, pressing himself against the mountainside with a finger and toe hold. "Say—we never in the world can get back down this way!" The sudden thought struck him with such paralyzing force that he almost loosened his grip. Unless there was some easier way down, Kurul and he might find themselves helplessly trapped on the mountain! "Oh, well," Dick decided. "I've got enough to worry about now!"

Up, up and up the two human flies went, stopping for rest on crags where they could, with fingers now bleeding from the sharp edges of stones and shoe leather cut and skinned.

"Do you think we're going to make it?"

Dick finally asked, with a note of despair in his voice.

"Sure—make it!" said Kurul, stoutly.

Dick, at a resting point, patted Kurul appreciatively on his sturdy shoulder.

"Kurul," he said. "You're one in a million!"

The lone Taharan frowned wonderingly but decided it must be some kind of compliment and showed his teeth.

And now the most difficult climb of all began with the end in sight, an overhanging ledge which projected out and to which they would have to cling on the under side with their bodies hanging over a vast chasm below.

"Go slow!" was Kurul's admonition as this last objective was reached.

Perspiration stood out upon Dick's body, not only the perspiration of exertion but an outpouring of sweat due to the terrific nerve strain of the moment. Cautiously he reached up overhead and clutched the limb of a hardy vine which had curled itself around the crag. Was it strong enough to support his weight, to enable him to swing his body out and over the edge of the projecting boulder?

"What you think, Kurul?" asked Dick, knowing that Kurul, just below, must be watching his every movement.

"Looks good," said Kurul, after a slight hesitation.

Dick waited to be certain that he was sufficiently rested to make the greatest effort of all—and the most dangerous. He did not venture another look below for fear it would unnerve him entirely. Only the thoughts of Ray and Dan and their dependence upon him as well as his own necessity for persevering, gave Dick the strength and courage he needed at that instant to make the attempt.

"Here I go!" he announced, finally.

Grasping the vine firmly, Dick swung himself out from the mountain side, much as an acrobat would cut loose on a trapeze. His objective was the reaching of the edge of the overhanging cliff so that he might climb up over it.

Sssssssnap!

It all happened so quickly that Dick had no time to think or to act. The vine that had appeared so rugged was dry and rotten, a section more than two inches thick breaking off in his hands! Dick's body started dropping and he shut his eyes, prepared to meet his end in the long, agonizing fall to the canyon hundreds of feet below.

"Master!" cried Kurul, hoarsely.

A strong arm reached out and encircled Dick's waist as his form shot past the lone Taharan. This arm swept Dick inward toward the mountain side and crushed him with bruising force against it, with Dick instinctively reaching out for some kind of hold. Both he and Kurul wavered on the brink of eternity as they struggled to maintain a balance. He felt Kurul's arm tighten about him as though Kurul, now that Dick had gotten a grip was himself in need of help to keep from falling. But Kurul's grasp and the shifting of his body weight was proving too much for Dick to hold. His own fingers were slowly slipping from the crevice. He wasn't in position so that he could reach around with one arm and aid Kurul for his feet had not, as yet, found a resting place. Suddenly, however, at a moment when Dick felt that he must let go, Kurul's hold of him was released.

"There!" cried Dick, greatly relieved.

"That's better! You all set, Kurul? . . . You saved my life, old fellow."

There was no answer. Dick, still gasping for breath and trembling from the terrorizing shock, ventured a glance down.

"Kurul!" he fairly screamed. "KURUL! . . . Oh, God! . . ."

Far below, turning end over end, was the stalwart form of the lone Taharan, tumbling through space much as the ill-fated Kurt had done, and destined to join his comrade in the land of the Great Beyond.

"He gave his life for mine!" sobbed Dick. "He knew if he clung to me that he'd drag me off, too. Poor, wonderful Kurul! It's the curse that got him. 'Within another week, another will be dead,' is what that priest said. Well, he's avenged his grievance on Kurt and Kurul who were the main offenders. And now there's only Ray, Dan and myself left. 'Within yet a third week, death shall strike three times . . .'"

Dick clung to his insecure hold in a frenzy of apprehension. A nausea welled up within him. It seemed for the moment as though he must give up, as though he could not again gain courage to attempt the surmounting of this overhanging ledge which kept him from reaching the top. He was apparently almost within reach of the Master and yet, if he could not overcome the final obstacle, he might as well have been thousands of miles away.

"I've got to do it if it's humanly possible!" Dick finally decided.

Slowly shifting his position, he crawled inches upward. Darkness had settled over the valley and deep shadows were slanting across the mountain peaks. There was no time to lose. He couldn't cling to the side of the mountain all night and he must have light to make his precarious moves.

"That vine still appears to be the only thing I can get hold of," said Dick, after a close observation. "This piece of it feels green and stout. It seems to be firmly rooted up above. It's my only chance and I've got to take it!"

With his heart palpitating wildly, Dick once more entrusted the weight of his body to the stem or trunk of the vine. His body dangled in mid-air as he worked his way along it to the edge of the overhanging precipice and then commenced pulling himself up, hand over hand, rope fashion. Nearing the top, a section of the vine was torn from its moorings and let him down suddenly, but it caught and held and Dick made up the lost ground, finally scrambling over the top ledge and flattening out on the rock, totally exhausted.

Recovered enough to sit up, Dick looked eagerly about him. Then his spirits fell.

He was on a rock ledge, perhaps a hundred feet across, a miniature plateau. Beyond, and separated by a gap of about fifteen feet, was another and higher mountain. In the side of this mountain was a cave, no doubt the abiding place of Bhagavan Vamadeva.

"But how am I going to get across the intervening space?" Dick asked himself. "There's a drop of hundreds of feet in that fifteen foot gap. It looks like I've gotten up here and trapped myself for I certainly cannot go down the way I came."

Studying the situation carefully, Dick saw that the two ledges, the one he was on and the one across from him, were about on a level.

"I might try to jump it!" he considered, and shuddered as he did it. "I've broad-jumped that distance before . . . but never at a height like this!"

Slipping off the carpet which had contained the amazing directions leading to this point, Dick divested himself of everything possible which meant an added weight. Then he paced off a distance back from the edge and practiced running to within a few feet of a possible take-off point.

"I've come this far," thought Dick, talking to himself to give him courage. "Why should I turn weak-hearted now?"

On a feeling of sudden determination, Dick dashed for the edge of the cliff and leaped off into space. He had a fleeting vision of a dark void below, night having blotted out the canyon, and his next impression was that of his feet hitting the other side, then falling forward heavily on his hands and knees and lying, stunned.

# CHAPTER XII

# THE ABODE OF THE MASTER

"WELL done, Dick Sahib, seeker of Light and Truth," a soothingly pleasant voice was saying when he had regained consciousness.

Dick opened his eyes and gazed wonderingly about him. He was seated propped against a wall inside a cavern which glowed with a strange illumination that seemed to hang in the air. Seated in front of him was a radiant personage, the kindliest face he had ever looked upon, a man of splendid physique and erect carriage, whose simple white attire appeared phosphorescent in the spiritual glow which seemed to emanate from his entire being.

"Bhagavan Vamadeva!" Dick answered, reverently.

"I answer to that name," said the Master. "And you have won the right to ask for Service in my name."

"Then, O Master," petitioned Dick,

urgently, "Can you set aside the curse in time to save the lives of Ray and Dan Carter? ... That's all I ask!"

Bhagavan Vamadeva studied Dick intently.

"You would not ask for yourself?" he said, quietly.

"Not if it means a choice between Ray and Dan," was Dick's prompt reply. "I'm interested in their safety first of all."

The golden glow in the room appeared to increase as though it were a spiritual rather than a material effulgence.

"Well spoken," approved Bhagavan Vamadeva. "It has been said by a greater Master than I, 'he who would lose his life shall save it,' and you, who would give your life for your friends shall also be spared from the evil-working power of the Curse. What has been done cannot be altered. Your two faithful Taharans have gone to their reward, having earned for themselves a higher grade of expression in the next life that they are to live on earth. But you three white travelers from America will be spared for I command the forces set in motion by the Curse to be disrupted, torn apart, and destroyed. I surround you three with an impenetrable armor of vibration too strong for the vengeful mind of the priest to affect."

"How can I begin to thank you?" replied Dick, almost overcome with gratitude.

"You cannot thank me," replied the Master, smiling. "This is not a favor—life pays each human back in the coin of his own acts. You have earned whatever has come to you or I, with my power, would be powerless to aid you."

"It is all unbelievably wonderful!" breathed Dick, tremendously impressed. "I have wanted, more than anything else, to satisfy my inner wonderment as to whether men of your high development actually existed. The beggar in Benares gave me the first evidence of it with his message; then the old weaver woman with her marvelous carpet designed for me: these two happenings gave me the faith and the courage to persevere until I finally reached you. But I would gladly go through my trying experiences again to have the privilege which is granted me now!"

Dick could sense a warmth of feeling which seemed to exude from the Master and embrace him so that it set his body tingling with an ecstacy he had never experienced.

"Dick Sahib has a fine willingness to serve and to learn," commended Bhagavan Vamadeva. "And I will raise his vibrations to enable him to enter the plane of vision, to be aware of what is taking place at distant points, to visit, if he wishes, his friends Ray and Dan!"

Dick regarded the Master with great eagerness. He thrilled at the very prospects of this revelation. If this phenomena were made possible to him, it would transcend television since television demanded a mechanical eye at the scene to be broadcast while he, apparently, would be able to direct his mind to a point and be conscious of what was happening there.

"Dick Sahib will relax," continued Bhagavan Vamadeva. "He will remember that the human mind is somewhat like the radio. Each thought has a rate and character of vibration. We think in terms of mental pictures. If Dick Sahib will make his own mind receptive and look within for pictures to appear, he may direct his thought to distant places, tune in on the minds of humans at that point and learn what is occurring."

"Do you wish me to try now?" asked Dick.

"You may," said the Master. "Close your eyes and look within. At first your mind may be clouded and the images may be distorted . . . but, as clearer impressions commence to come to you, do not rule them out with your conscious mind, but speak them aloud to me, no matter how ridiculous they may seem, and I will tell you whether or not they are true."

Dick did as directed. In the great stillness of this mountain fastness, it seemed easier to relax and to concentrate. He seemed to feel himself united with a dynamo of power. For some minutes nothing but random thoughts and impressions came to him as he tried to center his mind upon Ray and Dan.

"You are trying too hard," counselled the Master. "You do not have to make a conscious effort. The mental pictures come easily as soon as you have tuned in properly. Time and space do not exist when the inner mind is used."

Relaxing still more, letting go with his conscious mind, and almost entering the dream state, Dick was suddenly brought keenly alert by a picture that appeared in his mind's eye.

He gasped as he followed the scene, not able to believe it possible.

"Speak out!" directed Bhagavan Vamadeva. "If you do not describe these pictures as they come, you are apt to lose a memory of them. You are not far enough developed to hold them for long."

"Why," cried Dick, greatly concerned. "I must be imagining things but I see Ray Carter in the power of Raja Singh. I can hear her crying to me for help. She seems to be surrounded by Hindu maids who are preparing her for some ceremony. Good heavens—it looks like she's being forced to marry the Raja! ... This can't be so! ... Tell me, it can't be so!"

Dick opened his eyes to gaze concernedly at Bhagavan Vamadeva.

"Do not break the vibration!" urged the Master in an even voice. "Dick Sahib is doing remarkably well. Perhaps he can see more."

Shutting his eyes again, Dick relaxed, senses acutely attuned and intensely desirous of learning more about this astounding vision.

"Now I see Dan!" reported Dick, excitedly, after some moments. "He's locked in a room

with a high ceiling that has a little latticed window near the top of a side wall.   He's pacing
up and down and he's thinking of me . . . and
cursing the Raja.   He thinks I'm dead . . . that
I've been killed by the Raja's men.   Oh, now
I get it—the Raja's told him that he has ordered
his men to kill me . . . and Dan is to be shot
the morning that Ray is given in marriage to
the Raja . . . then the Raja intends to destroy
all evidence of our being there.   If our fathers
visit the Palace he will treat them hospitably
and express his regrets when they say they are
looking for us, telling them that our whole
party had gone on.   Ray will be hidden in the
Inner Palace which is inaccessible to Man
and . . . oh, Master—this is all a terrible night-
mare or something, isn't it?"

Bhagavan Vamadeva shook his head.

"You are seeing very clearly," he verified.

"Then what can I do?" begged Dick, horrified.   "I can't let these things happen!   The
curse itself couldn't be any worse than this!"

"That is true," acknowledged the Master.
"I can banish a curse easier than I can alter these
circumstances for a curse emanates from the
mind of one man and is often an abuse of

natural law and without justice. But here we have the lives of three people bound up in a human complication where karma is playing its part. And, while it is given to me to aid, Dick Sahib will have to *act* in order to save his friends from this new danger."

"I will do whatever is necessary!" volunteered Dick, starting up, disregarding his own great weariness of body.

"You will first sleep and refresh yourself," said Bhagavan Vamadeva. "Then I shall make known a plan whereby you may rescue the girl, Ray, of whom you are so fond. If you will but stretch yourself out on that couch . . ." The Master indicated a spot beside Dick which, to his amazement, now contained a comfortable looking cot.

"Say—was that there all the time?" asked Dick, breathlessly.

"It is there for your convenience," smiled Bhagavan Vamadeva. "Dick Sahib should not question; rather should he accept. He is in the presence of good forces. On the morrow he has work to do. Perhaps, meanwhile, he may visit Ray and Dan in his sleep. Who knows?"

"Who knows!" repeated Dick, intrigued by the idea, his heart going out to his two friends, now in the grip of this new peril.

Getting upon the couch, Dick stretched out as directed. He sank almost at once into a profound sleep.

Sunrise on the mountain top! An indescribable sight to be witnessed by few mortals! It was this to which Dick awakened, his whole being rejuvenated with vigor and hope and the desire to hear what the Master might have to say.

"I have no recollection of any dream," said Dick, a bit disappointed. "I guess I wasn't developed enough to . . ."

Bhagavan Vamadeva, who was sitting in precisely the same place where Dick had first seen him, appeared amused.

"Your conscious mind is the only one that is not sufficiently developed," he interjected. "If it knew how to contact the subconscious part of you, it would tell you of the visit you had with Ray last night, of your telling her not to worry, that you were coming to save her from Raja Singh. And it would also tell of your conference with Dan, of your trying to buoy up his spirits. But since your conscious mind was blanked during the experience and has not been trained to secure a report from your inner self, it has no carry-over impressions to give you this morning. But you did call upon your friends for I was with you!"

Dick, who had been staring, dumfounded, could only reply: "Well, I'll have to take your word for it!"

"I think Ray will remember," said the Master, "for she awakened after your visit, sobbing and calling your name!"

"I won't doubt anything any more," accepted Dick, awesomely. Then, half-apologetically: "I don't want to impose on you, Bhagavan Vamadeva. Were it not for the trouble Ray and Dan are in, I should like to ask permission to stay with you a limited period and learn much that you might teach me, if you would."

"Dick Sahib can learn just as much no matter where he may be if he but keeps the right attitude of mind," advised the Master. "One does not have to retreat to a mountain top to gain wisdom. You can attract right forces to you. If you will follow the instructions given you last night, you can think of me and I will be with you. It will not be necessary to climb the mountain physically again . . . you may do it mentally hereafter."

"That would be marvelous if I could!" cried Dick, fascinated at the prospect. "It is simpler than I imagined. And it helps to know that my inner self can do these things once I quiet the conscious mind and listen to the inner voice . . . or look for mental pictures that the subconscious is constantly receiving from different points . . . !"

"Dick Sahib absorbs quickly," said Bhagavan Vamadeva, evidently pleased. "I never travel far in the physical body . . . it's too cumbersome . . . I always travel in the astral or spirit body which you cannot detect from the material, as I make it known to your senses."

Dick gazed in admiration at this perfect specimen of a man opposite him.

"I presume," the Master was saying, "that you are hungry?"

"Well, *slightly!*" Dick admitted.

"Then let us eat!" said Bhagavan Vamadeva. A table with an abundance of choice delicacies suddenly appeared between them. Dick rubbed his eyes, looked again, then pinched himself.

"Question not," repeated the Master. "*Accept!*"

"Gee!" gasped Dick, as he prepared to eat. "I can never tell about things like this when I get back to civilization. They'd never believe me."

"This is not for the world in its present state of development," said the Master. "The wise man does not cast his pearls."

As fine a breakfast as Dick had ever eaten was consumed in silence. At its conclusion, he pushed the low table from him.

"That was fine!" he complimented. "I certainly . . . hello! Now where did it disappear to?"

Table and left-overs had vanished into thin air!

"Back in America they would want you to join the Magicians' Society," Dick grinned. "But I actually ate the food—or didn't I?"

"You *did!*" confirmed the Master. "There is only one Substance from which all things are made. By visualizing this food in its com-

pleted state I am able to accomplish all the
processes in the same instant. When I am
through with the Substance, I disperse it for
use elsewhere. None of the Substance is ever
lost, it only changes form."

Dick's stay with the Master, though to be
of short duration, was evidently destined to
give him sufficient to ponder about for the rest
of his life!

"And now," said Bhagavan Vamadeva, "to
speak to you about your own problems since
you live in a different world and must govern
yourself accordingly." The Master leaned
back and closed his eyes for a moment. "It
may interest you to know," he continued,
"that you were right in your suspicions con-
cerning Mahatma Sikandar. Your crystal
gazer friend has just enough power to be
dangerous. He yields to the temptations of
the flesh and refuses to learn self-discipline,
else he might be capable of fine development.
Mahatma played Dick Sahib false with Raja
Singh who offered the old crystal gazer a position as court astrologer if he would see to it
that you were led astray so that the Raja's men
might ambush and do away with you!"

"Exactly!" exclaimed Dick, marvelling at the Master's power of divination and pleased to get a verification of his own deductions.

"At present," Bhagavan Vamadeva went on, "Mahatma is returning to the Palace of Raja Singh, believing that both Kurul and Dick Sahib have plunged to their deaths. But his own magic has tricked him for he is only half right—he saw the impression of the fall in his crystal ball. Your fear of falling was so great that your mind sent out the mental picture of your plunge to death which was interrupted by Kurul who, himself, actually did drop to his death a few minutes later! Mahatma, however, could not distinguish between the two impressions because he has not kept his own thought pure and undefiled. Consequently he is going to the Raja with the news that Dick Sahib has been destroyed and the request that he be employed."

"That's great!" declared Dick, "then I can settle with him also!"

"Do not carry vengeance in your heart!" advised the Master. "If you do, you only continue the chain of evil. But you must also be prepared to meet physical violence since that is the law of the lawless order. Bear no malice, however. Act only in self-defense and act as I shall direct, timing each move to take place at the time I shall designate. This is most important. You must not permit a hitch of your plans because I cannot bind favorable circumstances together for long!"

"I shall make every effort to carry your directions out to the letter," promised Dick.

"Then will you listen to the only existing chance to rescue the girl whom Raja Singh intends to make 'his favored one,'" said Bhagavan Vamadeva, speaking slowly and concisely as though his thoughts were coming from afar. "A Brahman priest is to perform the wedding ceremony. You are to overpower him on the road to the Palace, leave him tied and gagged in the bushes and continue on to the Palace in his raiment. The Priest must be heavily veiled to enter the Inner Palace for his eyes are not to behold the beauties reserved only for the eyes of the Raja and this will enable you to hide your identity. The wedding party will be awaiting your arrival if you have executed this part of the plan on time and you will immediately, on coming into the company of Ray, the intended favorite one, draw out a bomb and threaten the lives of all, calling upon Ray to precede you from the Palace. You will so cow the Raja and his guards that you will succeed, if you have the resolution, in locking them behind doors, continuing on through the deorhis until you come to the Outer Palace where you should encounter Dan being led out by a firing squad. Here you may have to hurl your first bomb, annihilating the squad and liberating Dan. And then, if each step has been taken correctly thus far, aid will be awaiting which will take you from the clutches of a furious Raja and his followers!"

"Whew!" breathed Dick, visualizing his actions as the Master had been describing them. "I don't have much to do, do I?"

"It is a task demanding great self-reliance," affirmed Bhagavan Vamadeva. "Only one with a level head could be equal to it."

"But where will I get the bombs?" asked Dick.

"You will go to a shop in Srinagar and give the shopkeeper a sign from me," said the Master. "He will supply you."

"And how do I get down from this mountain?" queried Dick, still not certain of his ability to undertake such a prodigious course as lay before him.

"I shall show you the Way," said the Master. "You must have faith. My help shall not desert you unless you lose courage and faith. Unfortunately you still have to fight force with force in a physical universe. But one day you will reach a development which will lift you above such a necessity. Now we will go over the plan in detail so that you may get it fixed in your mind. The wedding is planned for four days from today. You had best return as you came, by pony . . . since Time will find you on the road in the proper place to waylay the Brahman priest."

Dick for the next hour gave his complete attention to the Master as he memorized every move he was to make.

"I have it now," he said, confidently.

"Then you are ready to make the return trip," replied Bhagavan Vamadeva. "And I will assist you down the mountain to the spot where your two ponies are awaiting."

Leading the way from his abode in the

mountain, the Master walked to the edge of the cliff and the fifteen foot gap which Dick had leaped.

"Take my hand," directed Bhagavan Vamadeva, "and make your mind receptive. Do not be startled as you suddenly feel yourself becoming light. Have faith in me and when I tell you to step off this cliff, do so without the slightest fear."

Dick took a deep breath. This was easier said than done. He had a memory flash of Kurul's body twisting and turning to destruction far, far below on the opposite side of this cliff. But the terrifying picture vanished and in its place came a peculiar feeling of peace, contentment . . . an airy lightness of body.

"Ready?" came the Master's voice.

Dick felt a slight increasing of pressure as Bhagavan Vamadeva took a firmer hold on his hand. Then, almost trance-like, he stepped off the cliff into space!

Stranger still—the law of gravity seemed to have been suspended! Instead of falling swiftly, his body and the Master's floated easily down, down, down . . . and then, at a certain level, commenced a circuit of the cliff, finally nearing a ledge . . . the very ledge where the day before Kurul and Dick had commenced their climb!

"Step" commanded Bhagavan Vamadeva, and Dick put out his foot, touching the ledge lightly and coming to rest upon it. "One moment!" the Master continued. "Before we break the contact, you must be your normal weight again."

Dick closed his eyes and felt his body grow heavier, felt the airiness leave him almost like a departing breath.

"It's wonderful!" he cried, as the Master released his hand.

"It is all in accordance with laws which Humanity has not, as yet, learned to operate," declared Bhagavan Vamadeva, smiling. "And now, Dick Sahib, courageous son of the West, I must bid you farewell. We will meet again in later lives and you will know, from time to time, that I am with you! The key to power is your Inner Self and now that the mystic has been awakened within you, use it!"

"I certainly shall!" responded Dick. "This has been the greatest experience of my life!"

"Your memory of the secret pathway to

my abode will no longer be with you," said the Master, "when you have reached the valley once more. But be not dismayed by this—Bhagavan Vamadeva is not in any one place."

So saying, the Master lifted his right arm in farewell.

"Goodbye!" said Dick, his heart overflowing with love and inexpressible gratitude.

But Dick's goodbye was addressed to the thin air for Bhagavan Vamadeva, he of the kindly face and God-given powers, had vanished from sight!

# Chapter XIII

## ALL HANGS IN THE BALANCE

A Brahman priest, journeying along the road which led to the luxurious Palace of the Maharaja Zakar Singh, was set upon at a lonely place by a lone marauder who stripped him of his garments and left him securely tied and gagged behind some dense bushes. The marauder, then attired as a Brahman priest, continued the journey, being welcomed at the Palace of the Raja by a special detachment of the military guard and escorted to the fourth deorhi or portal under heavy veil. The face of the Brahman priest had been concealed upon arrival and now, as he was permitted to pass into the innermost realm of the Palace, through the dim passages with their red walls, he looked neither to the left nor right but straight ahead.

At the entrance to the room in which the Raja had been married to his other wives, the Brahman priest was met by the Nazir of the deorhi, or personage in charge of the harem.

The proper salutation was exchanged and the priest was then led to the wedding party, a splendiferous array of lovely Maharanis with their maids-of-honour in support of the latest and loveliest of the Raja's favored ones, the young and most beautiful American girl, Ray Carter.

Maharaja Zakar Singh, garbed in his most costly and finest of formal attire, with bejeweled turban, stood beside the grave-faced, despairing but still defiant American girl who was about to be forced to renounce the world and to accept the all-powerful Hindu ruler as her Lord and Master.

Ray, despite her desperate situation, had never looked prettier. Her dark, curly hair had been brushed by her maids into shimmering waves, and crowned by a circlet of diamonds, rubies and other precious stones. Her softly alluring white skin contrasted vividly with the dark-skinned man at her side. The exquisitely colored and marvelously woven fabric of her dress added to the attractiveness of her shapely figure. There was no gainsaying that the white beloved was to be the most entrancing of all the Maharanis. Her position was one to be coveted by the prettiest women of all India and yet she would gladly have changed places with any and intended to die, by her own hand, rather than to submit as the Raja's wife.

"Ray!" said the Brahman priest, suddenly and dramatically, throwing aside the heavy veil. The lips of the intended bride parted in an expression of delighted unbelief.

"Dick!" she cried, and took a step forward, arms outstretched.

"Stand back all!" warned he who had reached the Inner Palace through a perfect enacting of the priestly role, a faculty taught him by Bhagavan Vamadeva, even to the proper words. "I hold in my hand a missile which means death to all!"

In his right hand, upraised, was a round, harmless-appearing object but Raja Zakar Singh knew full well its significance. A few sharp words in Hindustani ordered the guards and servants to desist for the moment else they be blown to bits.

"Come with me, Ray," Dick directed. "You go ahead, I'll follow. Out through the portal. We've no time to lose!"

Leaving the room with the wedding guests standing as though petrified with fear and consternation, the masquerading Brahman priest closed and locked the door, then hurried with his precious charge through the dim and winding passage ways.  At the third deorhi and the second, a wondering guard was caused to stand aside as the veiled priest, in Hindustani repeated the words:  "Will of the Master! . . . Will of the Master!"  And while the guards, with respect for the priest, permitted him to pass with the prospective bride of the Raja, inquiries were directed toward the Inner Palace to ascertain what the exact will of the Master might be.

"So far, so good!" breathed Dick to Ray. "Everything's been timed perfectly.  We must hurry for we are due in the outer Palace at a certain moment in order to save Dan.  The Master has surrounded us with good vibrations so long as we keep in step with the one and only Time!"

"I'll do anything you say, Dick!" Ray promised.  "I knew you'd come.  You said you would—in a *dream!*"

"I did?" Dick replied, and gripped her hand.

"Then the Master was right . . . he said I'd visited you . . . but I couldn't remember when I'd awakened. . . . Now—here we are! Don't be frightened, Ray, at what may happen. Just stay a bit behind me. If we're on time, we should step out of the Palace just as Dan is being led off by a firing squad!"

"Oh!" gasped Ray, but quickly controlled herself.

It was as the Master had depicted. No sooner had the supposed priest and the Raja's intended emerged into the light of day than they encountered a squad of guards marching a pale-faced but resolute Dan away from the Palace.

"Halt!" cried Dick, and threw aside his veil once again, holding aloft the bomb.

"Dick . . . Ray!" cried Dan, overjoyed.

"Release this man!" Dick commanded of the astounded guards. "Release him or it means death!"

But the guards, as the Master had predicted, gave evidence of defiance. Forgetting their prisoner, they turned upon this new menace and swung rifles toward their shoulders.

"Look out, Dan!" Ray screamed.

And Dan, jumping hurriedly to one side, started running as though his life depended on it.

Dick's arm came forward in the motion of a pitcher hurling a ball toward home plate. The bomb left his fingers in a direct line for the firing squad. As their rifles came to their shoulders, the bomb struck the ground in front of them. There followed a deafening, rocking explosion and a cloud of smoke and dirt . . . and the firing squad was no more.

Ray, Dan and Dick were all knocked from their feet by the force of the blast but were quickly up and running together toward the open spaces.

"The Master said, if we had timed every move perfectly, that our liberation would be at hand," advised Dick, as they ran. "But I don't see any evidence of it!"

"Listen!" cried Dan, excitedly, as they ran over the brow of a little hill toward the spot where their plane had crashed not more than two weeks before. "It's the sound of a motor!"

Stopping short all three looked hopefully toward the sky at a circling plane.

"It's our Dads!" exclaimed Ray. "I'm sure of it. They've gotten another ship and . . . !"

"We're saved!" declared Dick, excitedly, "if they can land and get us off quickly enough!"

Impulsively, Dick seized Ray in his arms and kissed her. She returned his kiss in the great happiness of the moment.

Occupants of the plane evidently sighted them and the giant bird glided down to a landing nearby. With propellors still twirling, Rex Carter, Dan's father leaped out, followed by one of the pilots.

"Don't stop! We've got to take off at once!" warned Dick, running forward, followed by Ray and Dan.

"Great heavens!" rejoined an amazed Rex Carter. "I wouldn't have recognized you in those get-ups! What's the big idea? . . ."

"No time to explain now!" urged Dan, "Get us in this plane, quick!"

The three were helped in as excited figures loomed up over the hill and shots rang out.

"Is the curse still on?" a worried Professor Oakwood wanted to know, as he greeted the young adventurers.

"No," replied Dick, settling back in his seat with the plane taking off across the ground and lifting into the air. "Whew, these priestly robes are hot! And maybe we weren't in a hot spot just a few minutes ago!"

"Dick saved Dan and I," recited Ray, taking a last glance down at the beautiful grounds and buildings of the Maharaja and shuddering as she thought of her narrow escape from the jaws of death.

"Don't you believe it!" protested Dick, modestly, turning to an interested Rex Carter and Professor Oakwood. "It was Bhagavan Vamadeva who saved us all! I can't ever relate some of the experiences I have had . . . but I was given a scroll of papyrus by the Master on which is written a message that shall prove his great power. I was not to read what was written upon it until I had completed my rescue of Ray and Dan . . ."

"Let's see it!" begged those in the party.

Dick, fumbling inside an inner pocket, produced the scroll and opened it with trembling fingers.

"Why, it's written in English!" exclaimed Dan.

And all, looking over Dick's shoulders, read:

> You are to go to the land of the Incas—
> Amazing Discoveries Await You—
> You will be led to finds bringing
> Light on Lost Civilizations—
> And a further Key to Self-Mastery!
>                               Bhagavan Vamadeva

"Suits me!" accepted Dan. "I've had enough of India!"

All in the party smiled their relief and expressed their wonderment as the plane, now at a safe altitude, sped them to safety and the horizon of new adventures.

* * * *